Going Down
the Ladder
of Love

Marla D. Jackson

Order this book online at www.trafford.com
or email orders@trafford.com

Most Trafford titles are also available at major online book retailers.

Printed in Victoria, BC, Canada.

ISBN: 978-1-4269-0956-6

*Our mission is to efficiently provide the world's finest, most comprehensive
book publishing service, enabling every author to experience success.
To find out how to publish your book, your way, and have it available
worldwide, visit us online at www.trafford.com*

Trafford rev. 12/11/2009

 www.trafford.com

North America & international
toll-free: 1 888 232 4444 (USA & Canada)
phone: 250 383 6864 ♦ fax: 812 355 4082

Acknowledgements

ॐ

I FIRST have to give honor to God. He is my real daddy and my reason for existence. I also have to acknowledge my parents, Elder Dave and Annie Jackson of Camilla. My brother, Marlon Jackson of Durham, North Carolina, and my four sisters, Veronica Jackson, Shanice Jackson, Katherine Byrd and Delores Pinkins of Camilla. To my children, Byron and Desirae, I just want you to get the best out of life. You both are the reasons why I work so hard.

To my friends at Albany Technical College, I thank you for your continued support and words of motivation.

I also would like to acknowledge my alma mater, Albany State University. Thanks for your support.

To those vain people who think this book is about you, it's not. Other than my family, I don't know anyone who was so great, I would write about them. This is fiction and if you don't know what that means-look it up.

Thanks to all my fans who kept asking, "where is my book?" Here's your book and I hope you enjoy.

Prolouge

ॐ

RUBY grew up in a fantasy world. Her life was never real or what is seemed. She smiled on the outside and cried on the inside. She was born with a twin, Randall, so she never felt that one on one love with her parents because she always had to share. She never really got to see what it was like to have somone to love her by herself. Ruby had problems, so she escaped with a fantasy life.

Ruby's first sexual encounter was with a guy she barely knew, but he told her he wanted her and that was all she needed to know. Well, her first real sexual encounter was with her uncle who molested her for eight years. She never told any one, but she knew it affected her outlook on life and especially men. Her uncle always threatned her that he would kill her father if she ever told. She believed him because she had been told by a relative that he had killed someone when he was younger. He stayed with Ruby and her family because his wife had put him out. Prior to her uncle molesting her, she loved him to death and she was so happy to see him every day. She would come from school and sit in his lap for hours until he start reaching under her skirt when she would sit in his lap. It felt weird, but Ruby didn't know if it was right or wrong. She was around nine years old and fully developed. He always bragged about how cute she was and how she was the prettiest black girl in the world. When he would say that, it made Ruby feelm like a real princess. She loved the way he made her feel by his words, but not by his touches. Ruby was blessed with a nice body. She had a round ass even as a little girl and it would shake as she walked. The uncle was thin, dark and his face was filled with scars. Ruby heard her parents say he had been cut in a bad fight some years ago.

He gradually began to have sex with Ruby, and at first it felt awful, but as it continued, it felt better and better. He would come in her room at least twice a week and it came to a point that Ruby waited on him to come. He would have sex with her so hard that sometimes her bed would be soaked in blood. He would tiptoe around and wash and dry the sheets before the next morning and no one ever suspected anything. Ruby was so confused about everything and she wanted to tell her mom, but her mom was so mean that she would find a way to make it her fault. It wasn't Ruby's fault, but who really cared? Ruby and her uncle had sex so often that she began to think that he was her boyfriend and he really believed that she was his girlfriend. He would watch her every move and when he wasn't watching her every move, he was trying to find out where she was and who she was with. Ruby was seventeen when her uncle found a new toy and completely forgot about her. One night, Ruby couldn't sleep and she was on her way to the bathroom when she heard some moaning noises. When she got closer, she noticed it was her uncle with her niece, Roshelle. Roshelle had just moved in with them and had been there for about three months. They were really getting it on and Rochelle seemed to like it-not like Ruby at all-who prayed it would be over every time they had sex. Ruby went back to her bed and she was happy because if her uncle had a new toy, he would leave her alone. He did leave her alone-he never came back to her room and she didn't know how long the affair lasted with her niece, but a couple of months later, Ruby was pregnant.

Most of Ruby's childhood was based on a fantasy life because that was the way she could escape her real life. She pretended to be rich and spoiled and the only child. She would talk to herself and play because she could be whoever she wanted to be. It was because of this fantasy life that Ruby was always left in the dark. She never really saw the life for what it really was because she was never in reality. To her, fantasy was better than reality. There was more fun when you could be whoever you wanted to be.

As Ruby became older, it was inevitable that she would have to grow up. She would have to live in the real world. Ruby's main problem was that she wanted to be accepted by everyone. That feeling left her alone and trapped inside of who she was really supposed to be. She was a great person, but she had no idea of how to let that out. She had sex, not because she was in love, but because she wanted to be loved. She thought having sex would make her loved and wanted by the opposite sex. She knew a lot of her sexual problems were from her encounter with her uncle because sometimes she craved sex like one craves food. She also had a terrible secret. Her son was really her uncles, but she blamed it on someone she had sex with in her neighborhood one night. He didn't really bother with Ruby or the baby , so no one really needed to know that her son was born out of an incest relationship.

A person has to find out who she or he really is before one could give to another person. Ruby lived over 40 years and did not know who she really was and that caused destruction to herself and to others in her life. Ruby tried to suger coat her life and that's how she ended up with Fred and all the other men in her life. Men had done her wrong, but most importantly, Ruby had done herself wrong. She had loved and lost and loved and lost and she was tired of losing. She had given herself to men who didn't appreciate who she was as a woman.

When Ruby marries Fred, she feels complete, but was Fred complete? Fred was very good looking. He was a big guy with a shiny bald head. He was sexy, and Ruby fell in love with him the minute she saw him. When Ruby finds out at 45 that she is pregnant, it is a different world. What she didn't plan on was her husband also fathering a child with his ex-wife. Is the ladder of love this hard to climb?

Fred met Ruby at work and he was in love at first sight. Fred knew he had to have her, but he had one problem-a wife. For some reason, when a man wants a woman, it really doesnt matter what the problem is because he will work around it. He became friends with Ruby and eventually they became lovers. Once they became lovers, he knew she would be his wife. His whole life changed when he met Ruby because she was everything to him and she made him feel that no other woman had ever made him feel. Fred had a wife who was nothing compared to Ruby. Fred told Ruby that he was having problems in his marriage before he met Ruby, so Ruby made him make a decision about what made him happy. He left his wife and he and Ruby became one. But men make stupid mistakes and he made a stupid mistake of sleeping with his ex-wife, Camille, after he married Ruby. As Ruby is celebrating the birth of her daughter, she finds out that Fred's ex-wife is pregnant for her husband. It wasn't that he was still in love with her, it was that he was a man and men do things without thinking.

Introduction

❧

Ruby was in a state of shock. After she realized that the woman standing in the door way of her hospital room was Fred's ex-wife, Camille, she immediately turned to Fred. Fred had turned a totally different color. He didn't even look like the man she thought she loved. "I wanted to tell you last night," Camille said. "Tell him what," Ruby replied. "What last night?" Ruby screamed and she awoke her newborn baby. The nurse came in and took Ashley to the nursery and Ruby began to sit up in the hospital bed.What in the hell is going on," Ruby said.

"Let me explain, but first Camille, you need to go," Fred said.

"Go where, you won't return my calls since you got me pregnant and this was my last resort," Camille said.

Ruby was going crazy and she could feel the tears running down her cheeks and she couldn't take her eyes off the man she loved.

"Baby, I need to talk to you,"Fred told Ruby.

"What is going on, Ruby asked.

"I went to her house to get some of my tools that I had left and one thing led to another," Fred said.

"It just happened so fast," he said.

"Where was I?" Ruby asked.

"You were out of town at a conference," he said.

"I don't love her," Fred said.

"That's not what you said when you made love to me," Camille said.

"I really want you to leave before I call security," Ruby told Camille.

"Me leaving is not going to change a thing," Camille said.

"Just get out!" Ruby shouted.

Camille left but not without telling Fred that he needed to be a man do the right thing. When Camille left the room, Fred began explaining, but Ruby was so hurt that it didn't even matter. She didn't even hear what he was saying. It was like her heart exploded. After everything Ruby had been through, how could Fred do this to her? She began to cry and she just wanted him to go.

"I love you Ruby and that's the truth," Fred said.

"We can and we will work this out," Fred continued.

"How can this be worked out?" Ruby asked.

"Do you know how much I love you," Ruby asked.

"Do you know how much I thought you loved me," she continued.

"How could you go and be with someone else and confess to love me," she said.

"I have been more than your wife and I have been right here for you," she said.

"What made you do this to me," Ruby said sobbing.

"I do love you and I want to be with you more than anything. You make me complete and this was a mistake," Fred said.

"Having a child with your ex-wife is not a mistake. More than that, she's huge which means you got her pregnant the same time you got me pregnant."

"I lie in bed at night thanking him for you and you turn out to be like everyone else," just go and leave me alone," Ruby said.

Fred tried to grab Ruby, but she turned away. He was still talking but, she could no longer listen. Fred walked out proclaiming that he would return later to see his wife and baby. He was even proclaiming that this would work out. Ruby was crying hysterically when the nurse brought the baby back.

"Are you okay," the nurse asked. "No, but I want to hold my baby," Ruby replied. Ruby looked at her baby and reflected on the last couple of years with Fred. She had been so happy. He made her happy. He made her feel like she was the best thing in the world. She couldn't count the nights that she awoke and he was just looking at her like she was a jewel. How could this happen? She was always there for him and he was always there for her.

"Oh God, is there everlasting love," she asked. "How could he do this to me knowing all that I have been through?" God, please tell me, how could he do this?" Ruby was a wreck. Not only had she just been through an enduring labor, she had found out that her husband had a child with his ex-wife. Ruby could not stop crying, and when she looked up Camille was at the door again.

CHAPTER 1

ℂℛ

"I know you think the worst of me," Camille said.

'But I love him too," she continued.

"He told me that he still loved me too," she said.

Ruby couldn't speak.

"I don't want to break up your marriage, but Fred has to be responsible."

"Can you tell me how long this has been going on," Ruby asked.

"For about two months," Camille answered.

"I never stopped loving him," she said.

"But he's my husband," Ruby continued.

"And he was my husband when you were having an affair with him," Camille answered.

Ruby couldn't say anything because she did have an affair with Fred while he was married and maybe this was her pay back.

"I knew when he would come home every day and talk about you that something was going on," Camille said.

"I tried to pretend that it didn't matter and that it would pass over. That was until he came home one day and said he was tired and he wanted out. We never had any problems before that. Do you understand what I am saying? You took my husband and now you want to say that I took your husband." Camille said.

"Fred didn't tell me the story like that," Ruby said.

"Why would he," Camille asked.

"He was trying to have his cake and eat it too," she said.

"Why didn't you fight the divorce if everyhing was so great; furthermore, it has been four years, why are you here," Ruby asked.

"I didn't fight the divorce because I didn't have the strength to fight for someone who didn't want me," Camille said.

"And furthermore, I never lost contact with Fred. He has *always* called me." Camille said.

"I just want you to go away," Ruby said.

"What you need to want is for Fred to tell you the truth," Camille said.

"You know, I don't want to break up your marriage like you broke up mine, even though I do love him and he will take care of this child," Camille said.

"I know that I would never trust him, so you can have what you stole from me," Camille said.

"I didn't steal him, Ruby said.

"I fell in love with him the first day I saw him. I didn't even know that he was married. I just knew that I wanted him. He was just so different, and I wanted him. I didn't go after him; he came after me. Ruby was crying hysterically. We were so happy that sometimes at night I wondered if it was really real, and now I know it wasn't.

"I never meant to take your husband and as I think about, I didn't investigate the situation. I just took whatever he said. I wanted him that badly," Ruby said.

By this time, Camille was crying and she just ran out the room.

"God, I love this man, and I thought he loved me." This is our baby and now someone else is having his baby as well. "I love this man, God. HELP ME!"

By this time, Fred had reappeared. It looked as if he had been crying, but behind him were Damon and Demi and Ruby couldn't let them see this.

"Mom you've been crying." Demi said.

"Yes, I am just so happy that my baby is okay and healthy," Ruby said looking at Fred.

"Oh, Mommy, you are so sentimental." Demi said.

"I do love you and I am glad that both of you are okay," Demi said.

"I am glad too, Mom." Damon said.

"Fred, are you alright, Damon asked.

"Yeah, I am just happy that my two favorite girls are okay."

Ruby couldn't look at him because she knew she would start crying.

Fred did love Ruby and he had made a mistake. Sex is a weakness for men and Fred had to admit that he loved women, but he was in love with Ruby. He watched her with her children and now their child, and she was beautiful. He had made a mistake and he hoped she could forgive him. He didn't love his ex-wife anymore, and it was just sex. Would Ruby look at it like this?

Ruby went home in three days and Fred and her had not talked the way they needed to talk. They stayed in the house for two weeks without talking about the situation. They didn't even sleep in the same room.

"We need to talk," Fred said.

"I am listening," Ruby responded.

"You have to know that I love you and just because this happened doesn't mean that I don't love you. I love you with all my heart and then some. You are my day and night, you are everything and I need you and Ashley in my life permantely," he said.

"I love you too, Fred, but you had to know what this would do to me, she said.

"You knew all the bad relationships that I have been through, why did you do this to me?" she asked.

"It just happend," he said.

"Things like this don't just happen," Ruby said.

"At this point, I don't know what to do. I know that I love my child and I love you. Most importantly, I want this child to have her daddy in the house, but I want to trust her daddy and I don't know if I trust you right now," Ruby said.

"You have every right to hate me and every right not to trust me, but I need you in my life and I just made a mistake," Fred said.

Ruby looked at Fred and she remembered why she fell in love. He was everything that she needed and for the first time in her life, she thought she was in love with a man who loved her just as much. He was so handsome and sexy. He was standing before her defending himself and Ruby was looking at how he still had the magic to turn her on. She didn't know what to do. He continued to try to make it seem like what had happened was not his fault.

"The bottom line is that Camille is having your baby," Ruby said.

"I know and I am going to do the right thing and take care of my baby," Fred said.

"How do you think it makes me feel that her and me are having your baby at the same time," Ruby asked.

"I know that it is an awkward situation, but this can be worked out," Fred said.

"Worked out for whom?" Ruby asked.

"I love you so much," Fred said.

"And I love our baby," he continued.

"I have been a fool so many times for men and you were the only man that I thought didn't want to make a fool of me. For some reason, I thought you were different. For some reason, I thought you really loved me." Ruby said.

"Baby, I made a mistake." Fred said.

"A big mistake, Ruby continued.

"Once my children and family find out about this, they will hate you and hate me even more if I put up with it," Ruby said.

"I just think you need to stay somewhere else right now so that I can think." Ruby said.

"This is not fair, our baby just came home and this is my house as it is yours," Fred said.

"But I want you to leave," Ruby continued.

"Maybe, Camille will let you stay with her, "Ruby said.

The look that Fred had in his eyes when Ruby said that frightened her but she held her ground.

"Look woman, I am not leaving and whatever we have to work out, we will work it out together." Fred screamed.

At this point, Ashley was crying and Fred headed upstairs to take care of her. Ruby had a very painful labor and was in a lot of pain even now. As she began to sit down, the phone rang.

"Hello, Ruby said.

"Hello, Ruby this is Camille"

"What do you want?" Ruby asked.

"I really want to talk to you without Fred and explain what happened." Camille said.

"I know what happend, you fucked my husband and now you are pregnant." Ruby said.

"Are you saying you didn't fuck him when he was my husband?" Camille asked sarcastically.

Ruby couldn't say anything. Is this what it means when they say you reap what you sow. Camille continued to talk and asked when would it be when Fred wouldn't be there.

"I don't know," Ruby said.

"Can you call me when he leaves for a little while and I'll come over," Camille said.

"You know where we live," Ruby asked.

"Yes, Fred told me." Camille said.

"I thought you lived in Dallas." Ruby said.

Ruby and Fred lived in Houstan.

"I did, but I moved out here about a year ago." Camille said.

The more Camille talked, the more angry Ruby became so she ended the conversation with the fact that she would call her. At that point, Fred walked downstairs with Ashley. She looked just like him. She had that red glow that Fred had and it made tears run down Ruby's cheek. She began to think to herself that maybe there was no such thing as true love and that all men are dogs. She looked at Fred and hate and love was built in her heart. She couldn't even speak a work. She just sat there and watched him.

"Look, we are going to get through this, but you have to trust me." Fred said.

"Trust you, Ruby said.

"I wish you knew how you have made me felt over the last couple of weeks," Ruby said. Ruby had been home for two weeks.

"The sad part is that Fred, you knew what I had been through in relationships, so why would you do this to me," she asked.

Fred didn't say a word. He just sat there holding the baby. The house was big and empty. Demi was in Atlanta and Damon was back in

California. They were supposed to come home for the weekend and Ruby dreaded it because she was miserable. She knew she had to tell them. She knew her son would be angry and Demi would be upset, but they had to know because she couldn't hide it. As Ruby was sitting in the living room thinking about how she was going to tell her children, Fred came and sat next to her.

"I know that it is hard for you to believe, but I love you," he said.

"How can you love me and be with your ex-wife. You knew about my past and how I have dealt with cheating men and you turn around and cheat on me," Ruby said.

"I love you and I guess you can love someone and still be with another person," Fred siad.

Ruby really didn't want to hear this so she got up and ran upstairs. Ruby cried and cried. She didn't know what to do. She wanted her daughter to have her father in her life. She was too old to do this alone again. She just cried and cried. She found herself picking up the phone and calling Nathan.

CHAPTER 2

ᐯᐯ

NATHAN had always been there for Ruby and that was a good and bad thing. Nathan was in Florida, but it was nothing for him to get on a plane if Ruby said she needed him. Ruby needed someone. She had only been home for two weeks and she was very sick most of the days because of the painful birth. She began to cry when Nathan picked up the phone. He could sense something was wrong.

"What's wrong?" Nathan asked.

"I need to see you."

"How's your baby?" he said

"The baby's fine." Ruby replied.

"Why are you crying," he said.

"I need you to come to Texas. I need you," Ruby said.

"I am busy right now and it would be in a couple of weeks," he replied.

"That's fine. I just need to see you here," Ruby said.

"Baby, I'll call you in a couple of days, but you have to tell me that you're okay." Nathan replied.

"I will be, I just need to see an old familiar face." Ruby said.

Nathan didn't understand what was really going on, but he knew that if Ruby needed him, he was going to make it to Texas. He had been married for some time now, but Ruby *always* had a special place in his heart. He sometimes thought that he loved her. It was something she did to him when she would touch him or even look at him. She had been so faithful lately that it had been awhile since he had seen her. Whatever the problem was, Nathan was going to Texas to help Ruby.

Ruby had met Nathan when she was in high school. He went to a different high school, but they had been on and off for over ten years. He wasn't that good looking, but he was a nice and giving person. He was medium built and brown skinned. He had an ugly scar on the left side of his face, but he had a great personality, and he and Ruby had great sex because he was willing to explore. When Ruby met Fred, she told Nathan that she wasn't going to cheat on her husband. Nathan always claimed he loved Ruby, but he married someone else and left Ruby alone. But when Ruby got married, Nathan wasn't happy, and he told her she would be back and he would be waiting.

As Ruby lie in bed thinking about what to do, Fred entered the room.

"Baby, I love you and I want our marriage to work." he said.

"How can I trust you?" Ruiby said.

"I don't know, but I want our marriage to work." Fred said.

Fred began to look at his wife as he looked at her when he fell in love. He did love her and he was truly hurting now because he felt he was about to lose her. He wanted to touch her, but was afraid she would reject him.

"Fred after the children go home this weekend, I need you to go away for awhile." Ruby said.

"I need to stay here with our baby," Fred said.

"I need you to go away, so that I can make up my mind as to what I am going to do." Ruby said.

"I don't want to leave my wife," Fred said.

"You left me the night you slept with your ex wife." Ruby said.

Ruby was hurt and she wanted him to get out of her face. She just didn't want to see him right now. Love is not supposed to hurt was the only thing ringing in Ruby's ear.

"Just go away, Ruby said. "I am keeping this between us for now but for me to make a decision, I need you to go away. I don't care what you say or what you tell your friends or famly. "Just go away." Ruby said.

"Okay, but for how long?" Fred asked.

"I don't know. All I know is that I can't solve this with you here and tell your ex-wife to stop calling here and respect our house.

"I didn't know she had called," Fred replied.

"Well, she has, so you need to talk to her." Ruby said.

"Can I ask you one question?" Ruby inquired.

"What do you expect me to do?"

"I need you to forgive me and know that I made a mistake and that I love you. I don't want to be with my ex-wife. I made a mistake and I want my wife and baby in my life."

"You mean two babies. How can I accept this child?" Ruby asked.

"I don't know. I don't know. I just know that I love you and that should be enough." Fred said.

Ruby was crying because the man she loved was standing here with a bunch of bull, and he wanted her to just forgive him.

"Your love should have been enough not to make this kind of mistake. You knew my past with relationships. You knew my pain and yet you walked over that and had an affair with your ex-wife. How could you love me?" Ruby shouted.

"I don't know. I just don't know," Fred said.

Ashley began crying and Ruby walked away from Fred, but not before she looked at him and told him that he needed to stay downstairs.

Fred grabbed Ruby and shouted that this was still his house and she was his wife.

"Was I your wife when you had sex with your ex-wife?"

"You can go to hell and rot there for all I care right now." Ruby said.

"You have some nerve to act like you have morals and values when I gave you my heart and you go and cheat on me and not only cheat-get a baby. You bastard. At least, if you cheat, you should use a condom. You showed me no respect by getting her pregnant because without that, I probaly would not have known that you cheated." Ruby shouted as she tried to soothe Ashley.

"Look, I am tired and I want to rest and I don't want to fight. The children will be here tomorrow and people will be everywhere, so we have to act like we are still married, but we won't sleep in the same bed tonight. That's a promise." Ruby said.

Fred was tired of arguring so he went downstairs to fix him something to eat. He had messed up. Women-men's biggest downfall. If only he had not allowed his bulge in his pants get the best of him. He had a great wife and he had really messed up. He knew Ruby had every right to leave him, but he needed her and he hoped she still needed him.

CHAPTER 3

ℭℛ

IT was hot in Texas. It was so hot that it seemed as if hot was not the right word. Fred was barbecuring because the children had made it home that morning. Ashley was just as pretty as Demi was when she was a baby. Ruby couldn't help but notice that she should be happy right now if it had not been for Camille. At this very moment, she hated Camille. The house was also full of some of Demi and Damon's friends. Ruby was glad because she didn't want time to reflect. Because of all of the people in the house, she didnt have time to look at Fred either. However, Demi saw something was wrong.

"Mom, are you and Fred okay." she asked.

"Yes, what makes you ask that?"

"The two of you look like you lost a friend."

"We just had some marital spat-its okay,"

Demi could tell it was more than that, but she knew her mom would tell her when it was time. She gave her mom a hug and went back to her friends. Ruby went upstairs to call Nathan.

Nathan had called Ruby's cell phone late last night, but she couldn't talk to anyone right then. Nathan answered his phone on the first ring.

"I was worried about you," he said.

"I couldn't talk last night." Ruby replied.

"Well, I am going to be there next weekend," he said

"That will be great." she said.

"Are you sure you're okay. Nathan inquired.

"I will be next weekend. I promise to tell you about it." Ruby said.

Three hours later, people had begun to go home. Demi was cleaning up as Damon, Ruby and Fred gathered in the living room. Fred and Damon were laughing and joking about a television show; however, Ruby was sitting there crying on the inside about how her life had turned out. She was hurt and she was in pain. She was about to cry when Fred reached over and grabbed her hand. She wanted to pull back, but his touch still had an affect on her. When he grabbed her hand, she felt his warmth, and for a few moments she forgot about Camille. She thought about her husband and her baby. She wanted it to work, but she was in so much pain. The pain she was revisiting was pain she thought would never come back. She looked at Fred and he glanced at her. She knew he loved her, but she could not accept this baby. The baby had to go and that wasn't possible.

Ruby excused herself to get some water. She wanted a drink, so she could relax, but decided to just get a soda. Demi could tell something was wrong with her mom.

"Mom, are you okay," Demi asked.

"Yeah, baby, I just needed to get away from the crowd." Ruby replied.

"It seems like something is wrong with you and Fred," she said.

Ruby wanted to tell her everything and wanted to just cry and let it go, but she knew this was not the time and she was not strong enough, so she changed the subject and tried to think of something pleasant. They both walked back to the living room and continued watching television.

Later on that night in their bedroom, Ruby and Fred began to argue again. Ruby was tired and she needed the comfort of a man, not the headache of a man. Ruby stood her ground and told Fred he had to go once the children left because she needed her time to figure out what to do. Fred didn't want to hear it, but he agreed to leave for two weeks in the name of business. Fred told Ruby that she needed to figure out what she was going to do, and that she needed to give him one more chance.

Ruby wasn't even listening to Fred. She was thinking about Nathan and how he would make her feel like a woman again. It wasn't right to think of another man to get over a man, but Ruby was so hurt right now that she just wanted to feel good. She wanted to let go and not worry about someone walking all over her. Ruby began to wonder if she was the type of woman who would be in a realationship,or was she meant to be alone and give out sex when it became convenient? Ruby was too old for this, and she knew that she needed to make some decisions which were best for her.

CHAPTER 4

ᏨᎡ

THE kids left early Sunday morning and Ruby was glad because she was ready for Fred to go.

"I don't want to go," he said.

"This is the only way I can resolve this," Ruby said.

"I love you, Ruby," Fred said.

"I know," Ruby replied.

"I just need to be alone so that I can make a decision," Ruby said.

Fred left and Ruby immediately called Nathan. Nathan was going to be in Texas the next two weeks. Ruby had a nanny to watch Ashley as she finally got a chance to get out of her house. She had planned to meet Nathan at The Marriot, and she was excited to get there. Nathan had arrived in Texas an hour earlier and was ready to see Ruby. Ruby stilled looked good. She was 45, but she looked 20.

"You look so good," Nathan said.

"As well as you do," Ruby said.

"So, I thought you were happily married," he said.

"I made a mistake and so did he," she said.

"Are you leaving him," Nathan asked.

"I don't know and I don't want to talk about it," Ruby replied.

"I came here to be with you and only you," Ruby said.

Nathan walked over to her and the heat over his body made her melt. He began to caress her neck and her body overflowed with juices. Ruby couldn't remember the last time she had sex, and Nathan was making her explode. She knew it had only been five weeks since she had the baby, but her body had healed and she was ready.

"I missed you, baby," he said.

"I want to go all inside of you," he said.

Ruby wanted him and she needed him.

"I will always be here for you," Nathan said.

He began to undress her as he looked at her naked chocolate body. Although Ruby was married to Fred, she didn't feel guilty right now. Nathan began kissing her from head to toe until he got to her special spot and he began to give her oral sex like he had been waiting for years to give it to her. It felt good and Ruby wanted him inside of her.

"Please make love to me," Ruby said.

Nathan flipped her over and entered her from behind with a hard thrust that made Ruby scream with pleasure. He felt so good inside of her that she was about to cry. He was pumping and pumping, and all her juices were flowing like never before.

"Please get this," Ruby screamed.

Nathan turned her over and grinded inside of her like he had not been with anyone since their last time. Both of their bodies were dripping wet, and Ruby felt so good she was crying.

"I want to make you cum all over me," Nathan said.

"I love you and I have always love you," he said.

Nathan was giving all he had right now like it was no tomorrow. Ruby was caught off guard by the love comment, so she decided not to let it ruin her moment. Nathan was giving it to her like no other and Ruby was accepting it. They made love for over two hours and then they took a hot shower together.

"You know, I have always loved you," Nathan said.

"I know you might not want to hear this, but I needed you to know," he said.

"I just can't handle this right now," Ruby said.

Ruby began to tell Nathan what happened and he just held her tighter and told her he would be there for her regardless.

"Are you willing to leave your wife," Ruby inquired.

"Yes," Nathan replied.

The answer caught Ruby off guard, and so much was going through her head. She couldn't think.

"Yes, I would leave my wife to be with you because you are the one I should have been with and since your husband has cheated on you and fathered a child, we need to be together and this is our time," Nathan said.

"Can we not talk about this right now and enjoy our time together," Ruby said.

"I just wanted you to know that when you're ready, I will be ready also." he said.

The two of them made love about seven or eight times and it was all good. This didn't solve the problems that Ruby were having, but she felt good and that was good enough for now. Ruby knew she and Nathan had great sex, but she didn't want him to leave his wife and she was still married and she had no idea what to do. She couldn't deal with Nathan right now because she had a husband to deal with and that was enough.

"I have to go," Ruby said.

"I know, but when will I see you again," Nathan asked.

"I don't know right now, but I will call you or come to Florida," she said.

"Ruby, I know you have things to work out now, but I need you and I want to be with you, so when you are through working everything out, let me know," Nathan said.

Ruby left and she was smiling all the way home. When she checked her cell phone, Fred had called seventeen times. What was she going to do?

CHAPTER 5

❦

Ruby agreed to let Fred come back the next week. She was so tired of him calling and she needed to make a decision She felt strange because she had cheated on her husband and she didn't feel bad about it. She was in another world and Nathan was the ruler of that world. She was on cloud nine, but she needed to get off because she needed to deal with Fred.

Fred was supposed to be at her house around 4 pm. Ruby had decided to try and work things out and just let her feelings out the window. She knew Fred loved her and that most men were weak, and they didn't know the effects of sex on women. She could forgive him for having sex, but she had lost the love she had for him. She knew that when she went to be with Nathan. Ruby had come to a time in her life when she didn't need more than one man because she really did love Fred and he broke that trust.

Ruby was preparing dinner and prepared to talk to Fred when her cell phone rang.

"I just wanted to hear your voice," Nathan said.

"Look, I will have to call you and you have to wait," Ruby said.

"I don't want to wait," Nathan said.

"Now is not a good time," Ruby said.

"Was it a good time when your body was on top of mine or as I was giving you all this good loving," Nathan said.

"Please don't start and I will call you back," Ruby said.

Ruby hung up the phone abruptly, and she knew she would have to get back to him. Right now, Ruby just could not handle Nathan's drama. The one thing that Ruby didn't like about Nathan was his arrogance. He was so full of himself. He was a good lover, but not to the point where she had to have him. He was just convenient.

Around 3 pm, Fred was at the house.

"I thought we agreed on 4'oclock," Ruby said.

"This is still my house and I wanted to see my daughter," Fred said.

Fred headed upstairs and Ruby just gave him an evil eye. She went back to the kitchen and began to prepare dinner. Thirty minutes later, Fred came down with Ashley. She was so beautiful and just the sight of Fred and Ashley together made Ruby want to work on her family.

"I want us to make this work," Fred said.

"Me too," Ruby said.

"I know I made a mistake and we will have to deal with the child and Camille, but I know who I love," Fred said.

"I love you too, Ruby lied. She didn't love him-well not the way she used to love him, but she did want her family together. She had raised a family alone once and she wanted someone there for her now.

"It's hard to trust someone who has cheated on you," Ruby said.

"I know it will take time, but I will never ever do this again," Fred said.

"You will have to be patient with me as I regain my trust of you," Ruby said.

Fred took Ashley to the nanny and came back to the kitchen. Ruby's back was turned to him and he walked up behind her. Her skin was so soft that it almost melted his hand. Ruby could feel his touch and she was beginning to sweat. It was always something about his touch. He slipped his hands up and down her body and then turned her around. He kissed her as if she was going away for a long time. His tongue slid in her mouth and down her body as he began to take off her clothes right there in the kitchen. Ruby didn't care because she was feeling his body right now and that was the only thing on her mind. Ruby's heart was racing and she stood naked in the kitchen.

Fred laid her on the island and began to kiss her from head to toe. He gave her oral sex like he had never given to her before. Ruby was so excited that she wanted him inside of her right then. But wait, Fred had other plans. He began to kiss her and love on her like he was regaining his place on the throne. He then lifted her up and turned her over. He entered her from the back and it felt so good that Ruby let out a sigh. It was a sigh that let her man know he could come back home. Every move Fred made seemed so emotional and thought provoking. It was if he wanted Ruby to know that he was back, and she could have all of him. Ruby felt good, and Fred was hitting all the right spots. As Ruby was about to climax, she noticed the nanny watching and masterbating in the next room. Ruby was so excited, she couldn't even deal with that.

Ruby and Fred climaxed together and the nanny had disappeared. They lay there on the kitchen floor naked and sweaty but pleased.

"I love you so much," Fred said.

"I love you too baby," Ruby said.

Fred began to say something else, but Ruby stopped him.

"Don't say anthing else, just take me upstairs and lets do round two," Ruby said.

Fred didn't hesitate. He took his wife upstairs and lay her naked body on the bed. He looked at her as if he had not seen her body before. He began to kiss her and whisper sweet nothings in her ear. Ruby wanted him inside of her so badly that she was aching.

"Please make love to me," she screamed.

Fred wanted to look at his beautiful wife, so he made his request.

"Please get on top and show me how you love me." Fred requested. Ruby was almost 50 and still had a knock out body. She was beautiful. She had beautiful chocolate skin, long beautiful black hair and her beautiful round breasts were in perfect shape. They were just the right size and the nipples were dark like chocolate chips. Ruby still had the perfect ass that walked when she walked. As Ruby got on top, Fred was in heaven. Ruby was moving side to side and up and down all with the perfect rhythm. She was making love to her husband. She could feel him so deep inside of her, and it felt so good. She was feeling good and she wanted to make Fred feel good, so she increased her speed as she rode his penis like never before. Fred was feeling so good that all he could do was moan. He moved with Ruby as they came to the perfect climax. It was so intense that Ruby couldn't move off him. She just rested on top of her husband's hairy chest and her satisfied body tried to rest.

CHAPTER 6

☙

THE next morning, Ruby and Fred awoke with pleasant smiles on their faces. As they got ready to prepare for the day, Fred told Ruby he had something for her in the car. Fred went downstairs to go to the car while Ruby prepared for her shower. She was standing in front of the mirror when she heard two gunshots. Ruby's body froze. She ran downstairs and her husband lay bloody behind his car with the trunk open. The nanny and Ruby began to scream. The nanny ran back to call 911 as Ruby went to her husband's side to comfort him. His eyes were rolling in the back of his head and he was trying to say something.

"Please baby, don't talk," Ruby said.

"I ....need ,"Fred said.

"Please, just wait 911 is on the way.

Ruby was hysterical. She rode to the hospital with her husband in the ambulance where they pronounced him dead 45 minutes later. Everyone was in shock, but Ruby was horrified. The detectives were asking questions, but Ruby couldn't speak. She had just made love to her husband. They had just gotten back together. What was going on? Ruby needed someone to come get her because she was lost. The detectives could see that they were not getting any where, so they told her she could go and they would come by later.

As Ruby was preparing to leave, Demi appeared.

"Oh, Momma what happened?" Demi asked.

But Ruby couldn't talk. She had cried so much that her eyes wer aching and she just wanted to go home.

"Momma, who would do this?" Demi asked.

"I just want to go home," Ruby said.

Demi took Ruby home and as they were driving in the yard, Ruby saw the puddle of blood and just began to scream. The crime scene investigators were all over her house and she felt miserable.

"Oh my God, what has happend to my husband," Ruby cried. Momma, it's going to be alright. Just go upstairs and rest ,Momma, and you will feel better," Demi said.

"I really think I need to go to a hotel. I can't stay here," Ruby said crying.

"I will take you, and I will come back and help out with Ashley," Demi told her.

Demi and Ruby left. Ruby was so confused. Who would want to kill Fred? Was it random? Did he catch a robber? What? How? She couldn't stop crying. She was so hurt that she could not explain the hurt. She just began to scream.

"My husband, oh my husband." What am I suppose to do without my husband," Ruby screamed.

"Momma, you are going to kill yourself. You will be okay, just don't keep crying," Demi said.

"My husband is dead. He was killed in my yard." Please give me my husband back," Ruby screamed.

After they arrived at the hotel, Demi gave her mother some aspirins and she went off to sleep. Demi didn't understand any of this. Was it a sniper? What was the problem? Was her mom in some type of danger? Everything was just one big puzzle and she didn't have any of the pieces.

CHAPTER 7

ॐ

THE next day, the investigators contacted Ruby and they needed to get a statement. Demi went and picked up her mother from the hotel and her eyes were blood shot red. She was still in a state of shock. She and Demi didnt talk all the way back to the house and when she got to the house and saw the yellow tape, she began to scream.

"My husband...oh my husband," she said.

The next day, the investigators told Ruby that Fred had been shot with a 9mm handgun and he had been shot five times at close range. They assumed that he saw his killer and maybe even had a conversation with him or her. "Do you know of anyone who would want to kill your husband," the investigator asked.

"Not my husband," Ruby answered. The investigators continued on asking Ruby questions, but she didn't really have any answers. They told her that they had processed all they needed from the car and the crime scene and that officers would be cleaning up and leaving off the premises in a couple of hours. As the investigators were leaving, he told Ruby that Fred was holding something in his hands. The investigators gave Ruby a black box.

The black box held a 10 carat diamond ring. Ruby screamed and fell to the floor. "He told me that he had something for me and he was going to the car," Ruby screamed. The ring was beautiful and it exhibited all of Fred's qualites that drew Ruby to him. Ruby was so hurt now, and she really felt that she had no purpose. She began to think about Ashley and how she would explain to her about her father. She began to think about raising another child alone and she was so devastated.

Demi helped Ruby make arrangements and people began to gather at the house daily. Ruby's son, Damon came in two days later and he tried to console his mother, but she was a lost cause. She was lost in the fact that she had lost her husband and there were so many unanswered questions. Demi and Damon basically made sure everything was taken care of because Ruby stayed in her room crying all day and all night. Her mom, June, came in and tried to help her daughter, but she couldn't. June and Ruby didn't always get along, but they made the best of the situation. Ruby loved her mom, and her mom loved her. They were so much alike that it caused them to clash, but they respected each other and they were always there for each other. Ruby was glad she was here for her now.

On the day of the funeral, Ruby had to come to the realization that her husband was gone. The family arrived at the funeral and as Ruby looked at the casket, every piece of life left out of her. She tried to uphold and be strong, but it was so hard. Ruby made it through the funeral and they had repast at her house. People were everywhere, and they were making sure they were telling her that she would be alright and they were praying for her. Ruby felt better by knowing her friends and family were there for her but she wanted Fred. Ruby never dealt with death well, and she certainly didn't deal with her husband being taken away from her without a reason.

After all the people left, Demi and Ruby's mom tried to make sure that Ruby was okay and that she had eaten. She had not eaten because she had no appetite. However, it was necessary for her to eat so that she didn't get sick. As she tried to eat something, she tried to think of who would want her husband dead. She just didn't understand and if it was random, what kind of neighborhood was she living in? The neighborhood was definitely a high social class neighborhood, so what happened? As she was thinking, the phone rang.

"Hello, this is Camille." Ruby was so much into another world, she totally forgot about Camille.

"I was at the funeral today, but I didn't get a chance to talk to you," Camille said.

"I am so sorry, do you know what happened," Camille asked.

"No, and thanks. I am sorry that I didn't see you today, but this has been so hard for me," Ruby saidl

"Is there anything I can do for you," Camille asked.

"No, I will be okay and my children and family are here," Ruby said.

"So, how are you," Ruby asked.

"I will be okay," she said.

"When is the baby due," Ruby asked.

"I actually have about one month left," Camille said.

"Look, I know I caused some problems with you and Fred, but that was not my point. I did love him still, but I made a mistake-we made a mistake. I did talk to him a couple of weeks ago and I told him that I was sorry, and that I didn't want to break up his marriage," Camille said.

"I didn't know you talked to him," Ruby said,

"Yeah, I just wanted to tell him that I was sorry, and that I didn't want to break up his marriage," Camille said.

"I don't think you could have done that because we loved each other," Ruby said. Camille just held the phone.

"Well, I just wanted to let you know that I am so sorry and that I am hurting right now as well, especially for my baby," Camille said.

"I guess the right thing for me to do is to let you know that I will be here for you if you need me," Ruby said.

"Thanks, that really means a lot to me," Camille said.

They hung up and Ruby thought it was the weirdest conversation she had in awhile. However, she didn't have time to dwell on that. She realized that she had not picked up her baby since Fred had died. She went to her baby's room where the nanny was sitting and rocking Ashley. Ruby got Ashley and realized how Ashley looked so much like her dad and how she wouldn't even remember him. Ruby began to cry, and she just didn't know what the future was going to hold for Ashley and her. It was a hard road ahead, but she has always done well with obstacles.

CHAPTER 8

ॐ

I T was peaceful in the house because all the family was gone and Ruby could finally exhale. Demi wanted to stay, but Ruby needed some time alone and she was ready for everyone to go. She had so many questions that she didn't even know what the answers were. It was very hard for Ruby to go out her front door because she would still see Fred standing there. Why would someone want Fred dead?

As Ruby was going through the cards and letters, the phone rang.

"Hey baby, I heard what happened," Nathan said. This truly caught Ruby off guard. She had really forgotten about him over the last couple of days.

"Hey, Ruby said.

"I am so sorry, and I wanted to come to the funeral, but I didn't think it wouldv'e been right," he said.

"I have thought about you, and I wanted to be there for you," Nathan said.

"Thanks a lot, but right now I don't know what I am going to do," Ruby said.

"Let me come down and make it better," Nathan said.

"I don't think that's what I need," Ruby said.

"I mean, just let me be there for you," Nathan said,

"I don't think that's the right thing to do right now, but I will call you," Ruby said.

"Okay, but remember that I love you," Nathan said. Ruby hung up the phone without saying good-bye because she didn't need this right now.

She had a lot of unanswered questions and she was still trying to cope with who killed her husband.

The investigators began to come around and call daily, but they didn't have any information about what was going on with the case. They had some clues, but they didn't discuss much with Ruby. Months went by and Ruby was beginning to get better and her childen and mom kept a close eye on her. Nathan was calling all the time, but she wasn't ready to deal with him yet. Ashley was getting bigger and Ruby had decided to teach a class at the local univerisity so that she wouldn't be at home all the time dwelling on the loss of her husband. She had been stuck in the house for a while and working would make her feel better so she could learn to cope. Nathan was still calling and Ruby knew she would have to deal with him soon, but right now she wanted to focus on Ashley and her work.

As Ruby was healing from her husband's death, her mother died. She wasn't sick or anything. She had a heart attack. Ruby flew out as soon as her dad called. He was a mess. Ruby got to Florida, and everyone was there, but Ruby was making sure her dad was okay. Ruby did all the plans. Demi and Damon weren't doing so well, but Ruby knew they would be okay. The funeral was beautiful and Ruby made sure that all her Mom's wishes for her funeral were carried out. Kitty, Ruby's sister and Ruby's brother, Randall, all depended on Ruby to help them get through all of this. Ruby didn't get to see them often, but they called and emailed almost daily. Ruby told them they had to be there for each other if they were going to make it through. Nathan's funeral business was in charge, but he didn't have time to focus on Ruby because his wife was around. He called several times, but Ruby didn't have time for him.

Ruby returned to Texas, and tried to get her dad to come back with her, but he wanted to stay in Florida. He and Ruby's mom had built a beautiful house and he had Kitty, Ruby's sister to take care of him. She went back to teaching and tried to heal. Teaching again was great and it let Ruby escape for a couple of hours a day from everything that was going on. The only thing she hated about teaching was grading papers, but she loved giving out her knowledge. Ruby was teaching American Literature and British Literature at the University of Texas. She had some very bright and innovative students who really seemed to have a desire for learning.

After teaching four hours a day, Ruby would make it home to see her baby. For some reason, holding Ashley made Ruby feel some connection to Fred. When she was holding Ashley, she could feel Fred's spirit and it made her feel alive. The nanny, Jennifer, had been so supportive and helping that Ruby had fogotten about her little rendevouz the night before Fred had been killed. Jennifer had been working for Ruby every since Ruby moved to Texas. She was around 28 and she was from Hati. She had lived in Miami for some years and had moved to Texas with her husband. Her husband physically abused her, so Jennifer left him and started doing domestic work. She worked for one of Ruby's friends, but she had to let her go because her husband was looking at Jennifer more than he was looking at her. She was very beautiful. She had chocoloate brown skin and beautiful black hair, but Ruby never felt threatened-at least she didnt think so. Ruby remembered the night before Fred was killed and they were making passionate love in the kitchen that Jennifer was standing in the door masturbating. So much had happened since that night that Ruby had almost forgotten. Jennifer came in as Ruby was sitting with Ashley and told her she needed to talk to her.

"I think I saw something the day Mr. Fred was killed," Jennifer said.

"What did you see," Ruby asked.

"I heard a woman's voice, but I assumed it was you," Jennifer said.

"What were they saying," Ruby asked.

"I don't know and I didn't look out because I thought it was you," Jennifer said.

"I know they were raising their voices," Jennifer said.

"Did you tell the police this," Ruby asked.

"No, I was afraid to," Jennifer said.

"We have to tell the police," Ruby said.

Ruby called the investigators and they talked to Jennifer. They wanted her to come down and make a statement. Ruby, Jennifer and Ashley packed up and went to the police station. All the way there, she was trying to figure out who couldve been outside talking to Fred. Who could he have been arguing with? It really puzzled her that her husband was killed in her front yard and she had no idea of who couldve done it.

As Ruby waited outside of the police station, she began to think about how she had slept with Nathan and realized it was a mistake. It was a very big mistake. Nathan was always there for her, but he would never leave his wife. He wanted his cake and ice cream and anything else he could get. He was a great lover, but she had made the decision to work on her marriage and she really felt good about it. She began to talk to God.

"Oh, God, am I being punished for my sins by losing my husband," she asked.

"I did love him, but I was so angry and hurt by him getting Camille pregnant," she said.

"I just wish there was something I could do," she said.

By that time, Jennifer was coming out, and the investigators told Ruby they were doing all they could do to catch her husband's killer. "We will not stop until we have whoever did this," the invesigator said. Ruby didn't believe any of his words, but she knew she would not rest until she knew why Fred ended up dead.

CHAPTER 9

☙

Four months had went by and Ruby was learning to cope with being a widow. She would go and teach her classes and then come home and spend time with Ashley. She attended very few social events, but she attended enough to stay on the scene. Once a month she would volunteer at a shelter for abused women. Sometimes Jennifer would go with Ruby because that helped her heal as well. Although Ruby missed her husband, she also missed the comforts of a man. She assumed she was not at that point in her life where she didn't need a man. She had avoided Nathan by brief conversations and small talk. She felt guilty about their fling before her husband died, so it was hard to try and be with him, but something had to be done.

It was fall break at the university and Ruby decided to go home and spend time with her dad. Ruby decided to take Jennifer home with her to help take care of Ashley. Ruby had decided to get rid of some of their cars because the memories were too great. She held onto the Lexus and the Escalade. She drove the Escalde a lot because it was easier to drive and easier to load and unload Ashley. Ruby and Jennifer and Ashley had a very peaceful ride to Florida. They were going to fly, but decided to drive to get the scenic view.

They arrived at Ruby's parent's house and it was just like heaven. It was big enough to be alone if you needed to and it was just right for Ruby to relax, release, and relate. Ruby had told Nathan that she was coming home, and he told her he would make some arrangements to see her. She wasn't sure she wanted to see him, but she was very lonely for a man's company and it would be nice to be around a familiar face.

Ruby met Nathan that night outside of Boca Raton . Nathan lived in Tampa, so they were assuming they would not see anyone they knew. They had dinner and decided to take a walk on the beach. Nathan was so nice that it scared Ruby. Not that he was ever mean, but he was different.

"I miss you so much," he said.

"I miss you too, it has been very hard for me," Ruby said.

"I know, but I am here for you, and I will always be here," Nathan said.

"I know, but I have a lot to deal with now. "I don't even know who killed my husband," Ruby said.

"I know, but I want to be here for you," Nathan said.

"I need you to be here for me," Ruby said.

"So, do they have any clues," Nathan asked.

"No, they dont know anything, and it is really bothering me," Ruby said.

"I don't know if it was random or did he catch a robber or what," she said.

"What have you done to protect yourself," Nathan asked.

"I have installed cameras that covers the whole premesis, so we can see everything now. It's just too late for Fred," Ruby said.

"Well, there was nothing you could do," Nathan said.

"I just want to know why someone would want to kill him." Ruby said.

"So what happened to his ex-wife," Nathan asked.

"She came to see me after the funeral and I just told her that I would help her with the baby if I could," Ruby said.

"You are too nice because most women wouldn't talk to a woman who was pregnant for her husband," Nathan said.

"Well, my husband is gone and I don't need to hold grudges," Ruby said.

"Well, I don't want to hold grudges either," Nathan said.

He began to kiss Ruby with a passion that she longed desired. His lips and face were so soft that she became arouse just from his touch. The wind and the water added to the passion that was burning inside of Ruby. Nathan began to kiss her from head to toe and all Ruby could do was moan. Nathan lay her down and began to undress her. Ruby wanted him so so bad that her body was aching. She ached at his very touch. It had been so long and she was about to climax without any penetration. This was explosive. Nathan gave her the best oral sex she ever had in her life. He literally licked her insides out and then he entered her as if their bodies were meant to be together. The sand on Ruby's naked body added to the intensity of the lovemaking that was about to happen. They were moving in perfect harmony and perfect rhythm. It was so good that Ruby stopped counting her climaxes after three. As they were about to reach the last climax, Nathan screamed out, "Oh baby, I love you so much, oh baby, Oh baby, tell me you love me. Oh baby, I love you so much," Nathan screamed as they reached their final climax. Ruby could definately say that was the best sex she had ever had. As they lay there, tears began to roll down her face as she remembered her husband. What a time to think of her dead husband, but she did. Nathan was so into another world that he didn't even realize that she was crying.

"You know baby, I would leave my wife for you," Nathan said.

"I really can't think about that right now," Ruby said.

"I know, but I want you to know that I would leave her for you," he said.

"You know I never wanted you to get married, and when he hurt you, he hurt me," Nathan said.

"I understand, but I don't want to talk about that now, so how about we just dwell in the moment," Ruby said.

"That's good for me too, but I just want you to know how I feel," Nathan said.

Ruby and Nathan lay there for what seemed like hours. They just held each other and made love one last time. It was good for Ruby to see Nathan, and it was really good to make love to a man again. Nathan dropped Ruby off, but not before he reminded her of how he felt once again. For some reason, Ruby believed him, but it wasn't the time. As Ruby walked into the house, Jennifer was sitting on the front porch. Ruby thought something was wrong with Ashley, but Jennifer was just enjoying the night.

"So, is that a friend of yours," Jennifer asked.

"Yes, we used to date," Ruby said.

"So, are you ready to date again," Jennifer asked.

"No, not right now," Ruby said.

"You are a very strong and smart woman to me and I know you will make the right decisions regarding your future," Jennifer said.

"I hope so, but right now, I can't move on until I know who killed my husband," Ruby said.

"I have to ask you something," Jennifer said.

"I know you saw me that night you were making love to Fred, why haven't you said anything," Ruby said.

"I didn't know what to say, and that night I really didn't care," Ruby said.

"I just wanted you to know that I didn't mean to disrespect either of you. Its been a long time and I heard you, and well," Jennifer said.

"There's no need to explain, and I didn't feel disrespected," Ruby said.

"By the way, did you enjoy it," Ruby asked. Jennifer felt embarrassed, but she felt comfortable talking to Ruby so she answered her question.

"You make love with so much passion, how do you do that," Jennifer said. Ruby thought it was funny.

"I make love to the person with the love that I have. If I don't have love for that person, I can't make love. I loved my husband and that night, I loved him with all of my heart because he had hurt me and I wanted him to know that I didn't want him to hurt me again." Ruby said.

"He really hurt you, didn't he," Jennifer asked.

"Yes, he hurt me, but I forgave him because I wanted to save my marriage. My marriage meant a lot to me," Ruby said.

"You know, you should get out and meet people. You are young and pretty and you need to have sex," Ruby said.

"The only man I ever been with was my husband, and I have a confession. I use to sit and listen at your door when you and Fred would make love and masturbate. The two of you had the most harmonious moans," Jennifer said.

"Will you show me how to make love," Jennifer asked. Ruby was totally caught off guard, and she couldn't say anything at first. She hadn't thought about Jennifer or anyone like that and her experience with Alice years ago was enough.

"Maybe we should talk about this when we get back," Ruby said.

"So you are willing to think about it," Jennifer asked.

"Yes, I am. You have been good to me, so maybe this is how I could repay you," Ruby said. Ruby got up and ran her fingers through Jennifer's hair and thought about Nathan. He would like Jennifer. He would like her a lot.

CHAPTER 10

 CR

ONE year had passed and Ruby was trying to cope with things as best she could. She was doing some free-lance writing and still teaching classes at the university. She and Jennifer had not talked about the situation since they left Florida, but they spent a lot of time together shopping, eating out and caring for Ashley. There were no developments on Fred's murder case. It seemed as if the investigators had given up, and Ruby was still worried about her safety. She had no idea who would want her husband dead and that haunted her sometimes when she was home alone. Jennifer had met some friends, and she would go out sometimes. Camille had called a couple months earlier and she had a baby boy. Ruby had not seen the baby because she just didn't think she needed to, but Camille wanted her to see the baby badly. Ruby agreed that she would make time and go to see Camille, but she never did.

Over the next year, Ruby and Nathan had messed around a couple of times, but he was going to be in town for two weeks and he expected to see Ruby every day. Ruby had planned that she would introduce Nathan to Jennifer and create a little excitement. It was Saturday and Demi had flown in to get Ashley to spend some quality time with her. It was perfect. Ruby didn't mention any of this to Jennifer because she planned on surprising her. Jennifer came in from jogging all sweaty and hot and Ruby was waiting for her.

"I think you're ready," Ruby said.

"Ready for what," Jennifer asked.

"You said you want me to show you how to make love, and tonight I have a friend who is very willing to participate," Ruby said.

"Yes, I am ready," Jennifer said. At that moment, Nathan rang the doorbell and Ruby was ready. One thing about Nathan is that you didn't have to prepare him for anything because he was always willing and ready. Ruby began to think he was born trying to get laid.

"Hey, baby," Nathan said as Ruby opened the door. Ruby was only wearing a silk robe and her nipples were so hard that they were protruding out at Nathan as if they were telling him to come and get them. He was ready.

"I have a surprise for you baby," Ruby said.

"I like suprises, what is it," Nathan asked. At that moment, Jennifer came out butt naked. Ruby had never seen her naked. She had a beautiful body and it was really the color of caramel. She had a very nice body with nice, perky breasts and her nipples looked like they were ready to be licked. Nathan had never seen Jennifer before because he had never been to the house and he was standing there with his mouth wide open.

"Close your mouth baby," Ruby said. All three of them walked upstairs and they began their night of love play. Ruby decided to let Jennifer watch Nathan and her and then she would let her join in. Nathan was always so glad to be with Ruby that he could never hold his excitement. He began to kiss Ruby as if he was saying thank you for everything. He kissed her with so much passion that Ruby almost climaxed. There was something about Nathan that Ruby couldn't get out of her system and the great lovemaking was a part of it. Nathan laid her down and kissed her body from head to toe. Jennifer was so excited that she was about to explode. Nathan then turned Ruby over and licked her from the top of her back to the bottom of her feet. Ruby was so much in a pleasure zone that she was about to cry. He then climbed on top of her and entered her from the back. It was so slow and good that Ruby turned around just to say, "don't stop."

Nathan was not about to stop because he was just getting started. Nathan beckoned for Jennifer to come over and Ruby began to caresss her wet and beautiful body. Jennifer was so excited that she was dripping from sweat. Ruby took her time and caressed her body and then proceeded to give her oral sex as Nathan was having his way with her from behind. As

Ruby was performing oral sex, Nathan was going deeper and deeper inside of Ruby. Nathan was definately turned on and Ruby was having a time of her life. Jennifer couldn't even speak. Before Ruby made Jennifer climaxed, Ruby turned over and said, "Now, give your body to Nathan."

Jennifer lay there as Nathan pulled himself out of Ruby to give himself to Jennifer. Jennifer was so excited that her whole body was jumping from Nathan's every touch. The boy was good was all Ruby could think about as she watched him make love to her nanny. He entered her and she moaned a light scream and he just continued to give her powerful thrusts of excitement. Jennifer climaxed about four times as Ruby sat in the corner and masturbated. Jennifer was so pleased that she couldn't even speak. It was best that no one said a word, so Ruby and Nathan proceeded to the shower and made love in the shower for another hour or so while Jennifer headed downstairs to her room.

"You know baby, I don't ever know what to expect from you," Nathan said as he and Ruby lay in bed butt naked and dripping wet from the shower.

"I know, I just wanted to give you a little surprise," Ruby said.

"That was a huge surprise and a great one," Nathan said.

"You know that I love you, baby," Nathan said.

"I know, but lets not get sentimental right now," Ruby said.

"I just want you to know that if and when you say the word, I would leave my wife," Nathan said.

"I believe you would, but not right now," Ruby said. Nathan and Ruby lay there until they fell asleep and for the next couple of days that he was in town, he and Ruby and Jennifer played with the love triangle. They had so much sex within those couple of days, Ruby was ready for Nathan to leave. It was great, but Ruby was no spring chicken and it was time to rest. After Nathan left, Jennifer nor Ruby never said anything else about that weekend. They went about their daily routines as Jennifer took care of Ashley and the house. It was a weekend that either of them will never forget.

CHAPTER 11

ɔʒ

Five years later and no news or developments about Fred. Ruby had conpletely given up. Demi and Damon had both graduated from college and Demi was in law school in Atlanta. Damon was still working in California and they came home frequently. Damon was planning on getting married this summer and Ruby was helping from Texas as much as she could. Ruby was well over in her 50's and she was beginning to feel it. She was still messing around with Nathan. However, she and Jennifer never explored with him anymore. They were not seeing each other that often because of Nathan's job as a mortician and he was in another state. He was still begging Ruby to marry him, so he could be with her all the time. Camille was worrying Ruby a lot to come and see her baby, but Ruby really didn't want to, and she was really getting tired of Camille.

Ashley was growing up and Jennifer was a big help to Ruby. Jennifer had also met a man, Coby. He was a student of Ruby's at the local college and they met at a club meeting that Ruby had at her house. They had been dating for about seven months and they were getting it on a lot. Sometimes, Ruby would sneak downstairs and hear them making love and Ruby would masturbate right outside of Jennifer's bedroom door. Coby was fine and if Ruby had been younger, she would have been interested also. He was tall, dark, and handsome. He was also very smart. He was about to graduate and had been recruited by several law schools. Sometimes, he looked at Ruby like he wanted to try her, but he never said anything, and that was fine for Ruby.

Anyway, life was just simple for Ruby and she was content to live long enough so she could see Ashley become a woman and she wasn't concerned with falling in love again or even having an affair. She cared about Nathan because he brought out a wild side to her, but she wasn't interested in being with him or any one. She was happy just standing outside of Jennifer's door and masturbating.

CHAPTER 12

ℭℛ

"I really need to see you," Camille said.

"What is so important?" Ruby said.

"I will really feel better if you see my son," she said.

Ruby didn't want to see him because she didn't want to be reminded of what had happened with Camille. Ruby agreed, but was very skeptical. She didn't want to see the baby. She was still trying to deal with Fred's death and the mystery of it all. Ruby was to go to Camille's house on Sunday, and she just wanted to get it over with, so that maybe Camille would leave her alone. Ruby decided to leave Ashley with Jennifer and she rode out to meet Camille at her house. When Ruby got to Camille's house, there was a Mercedes that she recognized. It was Nathan's. What was he doing at Camille, and how did he know her? Ruby couldn't wait to get inside to see what was going on. Camille answered the door.

"I'm glad you could make it," Camille said. At that moment, a little boy, who looked just like Fred, ran to the door. Tears filled Ruby's eyes, but she had other things on her mind.

"What is going on," Ruby asked.

"Come in, we have a lot to talk about," Camille said. Ruby didn't know what was going on, but she knew she wanted to find out.

"How do you know Nathan," Ruby asked.

"Well, I met her a couple of years ago," Nathan said as he emerged from upstairs.

"I am so confused right now," Ruby said.

"I met her on a trip to Texas and I found out she was Fred's ex-wife," Nathan said.

"You never mentioned that to me," Ruby said.

"No, I didn't mention it because I had to use it to my advantage," Nathan said.

"You are really confusing me," Ruby said looking confused.

"Maybe, I should get you a drink," Camille said. Camille walked off toward the kitchen with her son.

"Well, let me finish," Nathan said.

"I met Camille and she was very heartbroken about her ex-husband leaving her and I found out it that her ex-husband was your new husband and I began my plan. You don't understand how much I love you and that I have to have you. You never really took me seriously, and I didn't give you much reason to believe in me. I had to win your love back," Nathan said.

"I never loved you, Nathan, it was just sex," Ruby said.

"You loved me, you just didn't know. Anyway, Camille was so heartbroken that Fred had left her and she began a plot to get him back. "He was so weak that it wasn't hard," Nathan said. He then paused and gave out a laugh that made Ruby feel uneasy. At that moment, Camille returned with a drink and without her son.

"Where's your son," Ruby asked.

"Oh, he's upstairs with the nanny. I felt the adults needed to talk," Camille said. Ruby took her drink, which was an amoretti sour, and it was also Ruby's favorite drink. She took the drink to calm her nerves. Ruby didn't know what to think or say at this moment.

"Well, let me finish," Nathan said.

"As Camille began to find ways to get her husband back, I just laid low waiting for him to go back to her, especially when she became pregnant. I don't know what Fred told you, but he was coming and getting some from Camille quite often. I would videotape it and take pictures of his comings and goings, but I could never show them to you because I couldn't hurt you. When you called me, I figured it was over and that I would have my baby back," Nathan said.

"But you were so in love with Fred," Camille said.

"I took pictures and videotaped you and Nathan when you met him at the hotel. I showed them to Fred the day before he was killed, and you know what he said," Camille asked Ruby.

"He said, it was his fault and that he was going to save his marriage," Camille said with tears in her eyes.

"After everything that he had done to me, he still wanted you," Camille said.

"He was with me the night before he came back to your house," Camille said.

"With you how," Ruby asked.

"We had some mind-blowing sex and he looked over at me and told me that sex was all we could ever have," Camille said.

"I loved him, and he was treating me like a whore," Camille said.

"That's when I came in,"Nathan said.

"I figured someone had to go," Nathan said.

"Someone had to go," Ruby said.

"What does that mean," Ruby asked.

"Don't be stupid, Nathan shouted.

"Nathan was already in town, and we began to plan our revenge. I didn't go there to kill him. I went to talk to him and he showed me this rock of a ring he had bought you to prove to me that he was going to make his marriage work. Nathan had given me the gun, but we were supposed to kill both of you. But your dear sweet husband wouldn't shut up. He told me to go home and that he would take care of his child and even hit it every now and then if I wanted him to, but he was going to stay with his sweet, loving, and rich Ruby," Camille said.

"Baby, I didn't want to kill you. I wanted to be with you, but I thought killing Fred would make it better for us," Nathan said.

"Oh my God, you people are crazy,"Ruby said weeping.

"You killed my husband," Ruby said.

"No, I killed my husband,"Camille said.

"He gave me no choice,"Camille said.

"So, what now," Ruby asked.

"Well, I suggested we kill you too, but your man here wants to be with you. At this point, I don't care what happens because once I saw Fred take his last breath in your front yard, I became a happy woman," Camille said.

Ruby slapped Camille without even thinking. Camille slapped her back and they began to wrestle and calling each other names.

"Look, women, this is not going to solve anything," Nathan said.

"You two are some sick bastards. You both wanted to be with someone who didn't want to be with you, so you decided to kill somebody, you are sick," Ruby screamed. Ruby began to run to the door, but Nathan stopped her.

"Look, bitch, I have tried to be nice, but you give me no choice," Nathan said.

Nathan grabbed Ruby from behind and took her to the den which was located at the back of the house. He told Camille to get the nanny and the boy out of the house. Ruby was screaming and yelling, so Nathan slapped her. He slapped her so hard she fell down. Ruby began to think of Ashley and sat quietly on the floor.

"Look, don't kill me, I have a daughter to raise," Ruby said.

"I don't want to kill you, but I want you to know that you can't go around hurting people when you get ready," Nathan said.

"How could I hurt you? You married someone and you are still married," Ruby said.

"I would have divorced her in a minute if you wouldv'e given me the word," Nathan said.

"I never wanted you like that. I thought we just had great sex," Ruby said.

"There is no great sex without love," Nathan said. He was pacing back and forth trying to figure out what to do. Camille had told the nanny to take her son, Fred, Jr., to the amusement park.

"What are we going to do," Camille asked Nathan.

"We are going to have a little fun and send her on her way," Nathan said.

"We have to kill her because she knows what we have done," Camille said.

"I won't tell anyone, I just want to be here for my daughter," Ruby said as she tried to get off the floor. Nathan quickly slapped her again, and Ruby fell back to the floor.

"Shut up, and let me think," Nathan said.

"You could've easily stopped this by just leaving Fred and being my wife or never marrying him," Nathan said.

"I loved you so much and you just brushed me off," Nathan said.

"I didn't brush you off, it was sex," Ruby said.

"Sex is love," Nathan screamed. He began to snatch Ruby's clothes off and he kicked her over.

"What are you doing," Camille asked.

"Come on baby and lets give her something she won't forget," Nathan said. They began to undress themselves and rip off Ruby's clothes. Ruby just lay there motionless just hoping they allowed her to live. They raped her over and over until Ruby's body was in a state of shock. Nathan had sex with her over and over again while Camille gave her oral sex. After they finished with Ruby, they began to have sex with each other. Ruby was so hurt that she was lying there crying in a state of confusion.

"You can get up and go," Nathan said.

"I don't have to tell you that you will not tell anyone what happened today because we will kill you and Ashley. We will kill Ashley first so that you wish you were dead," Nathan said. Ruby got up and went towards the bathroom, but Camille stopped her.

"Here's a robe, now get the hell out of my house," Camille said laughing. Ruby ran out of the house to her Lexus.

She drove home slower than she has ever driven in her life. She was so hurt and confused and she felt awful. She cried all the way home. She finally got home and ran immediately upstairs to her shower. She cried the whole time in the shower as she tried to wash Nathan and Camille's smells off her body. After her shower, she tried to digest what had happened to her, but none of it made sense. Nathan and Camille were crazy and they had killed her husband for no reason. She looked on her finger at the rock her husband was holding when he was killed. She just broke out and cried. Nathan had mistken good sex for love. It was a very reversible role. Its usually the woman who is confused. Ruby had allowed her sexual desires for another person get her husband killed.

Ruby couldn't tell anyone because she believed that Nathan and Camille would keep their word. All she really had was Ashley, Demi, and Damon. She lay on the bed and tried to decide what to do. She needed to get out of Texas. Ruby decided to move to California. Her son was getting married in a couple of months and that would be perfect. Ruby made plans to move. She found a beautiful home, and Damon was so glad that she was moving close to him. Ruby's dad died a couple of days before Damon's wedding. The family flew out to the funeral, and it was very hard. He had lived to be 94, and he was in a lot of pain in his last days. Ruby had hired him a private nurse, and she would call Ruby every day to give her an update. All he ever talked about was June. He was ready to go home and be with her. Ruby flew in and flew out of Florida immediately after the service because she did not want to see Nathan.

CHAPTER 13

ↅↄ

Aᴄᴛᴇʀ the ordeal with Nathan and Camille, Ruby was disgusted with life. She had no motivation to continue. How could someone so close to you, do the things they had done to her? She did not understand. She had done a lot of evil in her life, but she didn't deserve to have the one man she loved taken away from her. Ruby didn't believe in love after this and begin to just live to live. She was in California and trying to help Damon with his wedding. She was excited about seeing her son getting married. In her mind, she thought at least someone should be happy. Jennifer had moved with Ruby and she helped her a lot as well.

Damon's wedding was beautiful and so was his wife. Her name was Sheila and she was from Arizona. She was mixed. Her dad was white and her mom was black. The dad was a typical white man, but he knew Damon loved his daughter and that was enough. Damon really seemed happy and it was good for Ruby to be around her family and friends.

After the wedding, Ruby decided to move to California to get away from Texas. Damon was excited for his mom and she started working at the University of California. She was the dean of English and Modern Languages and teaching some classes when needed. She liked California and her time was up in Texas.

Ruby was hoping to never see Nathan or Camille again, but Nathan still called her cell phone. Ruby was completely at a point where she didn't want to have any one. Ruby began to concentrate on her work and her writing. She had begun to work out almost three times a week and she was looking better than ever. One day at the gym, a young guy approached Ruby.

"You look very good," he said. Ruby tried to ignore him, but he just stood there and examined her.

"Thanks," Ruby replied.

"What is your name," he asked.

"Look, I have been hurt, lost, trampled over, and right now I am damaged goods. I don't want to be rude, but I don't want to be bothered," Ruby shouted.

"I can dig that. At least let me introduce myself and be your friend," he said. Ruby had to admit he was fine, but she just didn't want to be bothered.

"Okay, what is your name," she asked.

"My name is Simon and I believe I have taken one of your classes at the college before," he said.

"I am so sorry. I don't mean to be rude, but I have just gone through a lot lately," Ruby said.

"I understand, but you were too pretty to go unnoticed," he said. Ruby continued her work out and was heading to the shower when Simon appeared in front of her.

"Just let me take you out for a drink," he said.

"Maybe another time, but not tonight," Ruby said.

Simon was a gentleman and he told Ruby that he was going to hold her to it. Ruby showered and left the gym, but there was something on her mind—Simon. He was good looking. It doesn't matter what a woman goes through when she likes men, she just likes men. Ruby liked men. Simon was about 6'6 and tall, dark, and handsome. He had this deep voice that almost made Ruby fall off the treadmill. He was something, but Ruby just felt she was too old to do this again.

The next day at work, Ruby was working on some grants for the college, when there was a knock on the door. It was Simon.

"I have been thinking about you all night," Simon said.

"Close the door," Ruby said.

"You caught my eye the first day that I saw you and I have never forgotten the day that I saw you standing in the classroom and I have tried to see you in town before." Simon said.

"You are a student here," Ruby asked.

"Yes, but not your student," Simon said.

Simon was on the game and he had an answer for every question that Ruby shot to him.

"What is it that caught your eye," Ruby asked.

"You have a unique sex appeal that I can't really explain," he said.

"So do you," Ruby said. For some reason, Ruby knew this was wrong. Simon was still in college and she had a PhD and was a full-time professor and an administrator. What did he have to offer?

"So, what is unique," Ruby asked.

"Let me take you out, and really explain," Simon said.

"I tried to tell you at the gym that I am damaged goods," Ruby said.

"Are you married," Simon asked.

"I am widowed," Ruby said.

"Well, you need someone to make you feel better," Simon said. Ruby knew this was not right, but in her mind, she wanted to explore Simon even if it was just sex.

"I have been widowed for awhile now," Ruby said.

"Let's exchange numbers, and go from there," Ruby said. They exchanged numbers and Simon left. Ruby sat in her office and watched from her window as he walked across the campus. He was good looking, but Ruby was scared. Her mind or body was not healed from what Nathan and Camille had done to her, but she still desired to be loved.

Simon called a couple of times over the next few days, but Ruby was not ready yet. She was having nightmares from what Nathan and Camille had done to her, and she just felt she was about to lose her mind. On Saturday, Ruby was doing her routine work out and Simon stepped up to her on the treadmill.

"I wish you would have told me you were going to ignore me," he said.

"I am not ignoring you, I just don't know what I want right now, and I don't want to lead you on," Ruby said.

"I am old and I have grown children and I have a baby." she said."

"You are not old, and you look better than most women who are my age," Simon said.

"What do you want from me?" Ruby asked.

"I want to hold you in my arms and let you know what it feels like to be loved," Simon said.

Ruby got chills down her spine and she longed to be loved with no strings attached. She felt it was her time. For so long, she had made sure everyone else was okay, and now it was time for her to be okay. She just knew that Simon was not good for her, but that he would be good to her.

"Meet me in the back when you finish," Simon said. Simon walked off and didn't even give Ruby a chance to respond. She watched his muscular body and he walked away and a certain heat fell over her body. Ruby did not know what to do, but she knew she had to do something.

As Ruby's time ended on the treadmill, she was beginning to feel a little nervous. She was thinking to herself that she shouldn't do this, but she wanted to. She knew that whatever Simon had up his sleeve in the back was not going to be good for her in the long run. She walked slowly toward the back and she realized that only two other people were in the gym. She called her nanny, Jennifer, to check on the baby and proceeded toward the back. When she got close to the hot tub area, Simon stepped out.

"Let me show you what you need," Simon said as he grabbed Ruby's hand.

"I am so scared," she said.

"Why, I am going to be very gentle with you," Simon said. Simon walked Ruby into the hot tub area and locked the door. He began dazing in Ruby's eyes and the heat from the hot tub and the heat from her body was about to make her explode.

Simon began to caress Ruby's face with a gentle stroke as he ran his fingers through her hair. Her body was trembling, so he told her to calm down. He then took off her shirt as Ruby reminded him that she had not taken a shower. Simon didn't care. He turned her around and unfastened her bra and then he just ran his big chocolate hands across her body. He turned her back around and slid her shorts down and he gently eased her underwear off. Ruby was so turned on that she couldn't speak. Simon didn't care because he didn't want her to talk.

"I want you so bad," Simon whispered.

"I want you too," Ruby said. Simon began to kiss her so passionately that Ruby just calmed down and let go. Simon led her naked body to the hot tub and turned her around as her back was facing him. He slid in from behind and it felt so good that again Ruby couldn't speak. Simon began to lightly stroke Ruby as if every inch of her wanted him. She did want him and when he moved, she moved and he was so well endowed that Ruby felt she was in heaven. Simon turned her over and entered her from the front and it was once again like heaven. They both climaxed together and Ruby just gave out a sigh of relief. Simon helped her get out the hot tub and told her that he just had the best sex he ever had. Ruby was still in a state of shock and really couldn't speak. She walked down to the shower and tried to forget what had just happened. What had Ruby done?

CHAPTER 14

☙

THE next day at work, Ruby couldn't concentrate because she was thinking about Simon and what happened the night before. She had tons of papers to grade, but she couldn't concentrate. As Ruby was beginning to leave for lunch, Simon walked in her door.

"I have been thinking about you all day and I had to see you," he said.

"I don't think what we did was right since you are a student here," Ruby said.

"I am not your student, so why should it matter," Simon said.

"I am sure there is some rule that will get us both in trouble," Ruby said. Simon closed the door and grabbed Ruby and told her he was willing to take the chance. He began kissing her, but Ruby stopped him and told him that her office was not the right place.

"I was about to go to lunch," Ruby said.

"Would you like to join me," Ruby continued.

"I would, but my money is low now," Simon said. Ruby told him that she had it.

They went out the building and got into her car and drove to a local restaurant and ordered lunch. Simon began to tell Ruby about losing in his job at the local tire plant and that he was coming back to school to get his life together.

Ruby was thinking that this was not going to get involved with someone who was "getting his life together." She listened as Simon was telling his life story, but she had made up her mind that she would be through with him once lunch was over.

As they were riding in the car, Simon told Ruby that he would love to see her again. She told him that she didn't know if that was a good idea, but they could see. Ruby felt like she wouldn't mind sleeping with him, but nothing more.

Ruby thought when they got back on campus, Simon would go away. However, he followed her to her office and he began just talking about himself. Ruby knew he was talking to three other women: An African girl, Shay, a girl in his apartment complex, Lacy, and a girl who owned a beauty salon; Kim.

"I am just talking to these women, and messing around every now and then," Simon said.

"I really do want a serious relationship with the right person," Simon said.

"I don't think we would work," Ruby said.

"I know, but I would love to be your friend," Simon said.

"Well that can be worked out, but you really need to go because I have a lot of work to do," Ruby said.

Simon left, but not before he gave Ruby a whopper of a kiss. Ruby was very much sexually attracted to this man, but she felt there was some danger here so she just decided to finish her work for the day and go home to see her daughter.

As Ruby was on the way home, Simon called and they talked from the college to her house which was about a 40 minute drive. Ruby had to admit that she enjoyed talking to him, but she knew that where she was in her life, she couldn't carry a load of a person who was about to start over. When Ruby got home, she got off the phone, and she went in the house and made dinner for the nanny Jennifer and herself.

By time Ruby was settling in for the night, Simon called and they talked the night away. They had a lot of things in common such as they liked some of the same T.V. shows, and they both liked to travel. But as Ruby was drifting away, she was just thinking about the night at the gym. It was awesome, but she felt that she was too old to go through all this again.

The next morning, Ruby prepared breakfast and spent some time with her baby and chatted with Jennifer. As Ruby was preparing to get in her car, Simon called.

"Good morning beautiful," Simon said.

"Hey, how are you," Ruby said.

"I just wanted to hear your voice this morning," Simon said.

"I am glad to hear from you too," Ruby said.

"I was wondering if we could go to lunch today," Simon asked.

"Well, I have a busy schedule today, but I will try," Ruby said.

"Well, if you can, let's go around one," Simon said.

Ruby was thinking it was a bad idea to see this man again, but she did like him and she could deny that. She taught her two classes and was headed to her office when she saw Simon.

"So, have you thought about lunch today," Simon asked.

"Let's go to my office," Ruby said. She did not want anyone in the hall listening to their conversation.

"Listen, we have to be careful," Ruby said.

"I forgot. It's just that when I see you, I get excited," Simon said.

"Where do you want to go," Ruby asked.

"I feel like barbeque if you don't mind," Simon said.

"That sounds good," Ruby said.

They went in Ruby's Lexus to this locally owed barbeque place and had a great time over lunch. When the waitress brought the ticket, Simon began his sorrowful talking about all his bills and money problems. Ruby was furious inside not because she couldn't pay for it, but because he had invited her to lunch. She paid the bill and tried to hurry back to campus. His conversation on the way back was not so intriguing. When they got back to campus, Ruby told Simon she had a workshop to prepare for and she would call him later.

Ruby got to her office and breathed a sigh of relief. She could not believe he called her and asked her to lunch and didn't have any money. One thing Ruby didn't have time for was a broke man. She had no intentions of talking to him again. Through all of this, Jennifer got married to one of Ruby's students. They moved to New Orleans and they were doing fine. Ruby needed a new nanny, but she knew Jennifer would be hard to replace, so Ruby and Damon worked things out to handle Ashley.

CHAPTER 15

ᘓ

Ruby ignored Simon's call for about three days and she avoided him on campus. One day, she was eating in the cafeteria on campus and Simon came up.

"I have been trying to call you," Simon said.

"I have been busy," Ruby said.

"I really like you," Simon said. Ruby didn't respond.

"I really want to spend time with you and get to know you better," Simon said.

"Well, you have a lot of women friends, and I don't play seconds," Ruby said.

"I want to get to know you better," Simon said.

"I have been through so much that I am not good for anyone right now. My husband was killed and I am not just good for any one," Ruby said.

"Give me a chance to make you happy," Simon said.

It had been a long time since Ruby had been happy since everything that had happened with Fred and all the crazy things that Nathan and Camille had put her through.

"Let's just take one day at a time. How about you come over tonight for dinner," she said.

"That sounds good, what about seven," Simon asked.

Ruby went home after work and prepared dinner. She made roast beef, rice and gravy , green peas, and dinner rolls. She even made a cake for dessert. Jennifer had met one of Ruby's students and was out for the night. Ashley was with one of Ruby's cousins for the night, so the night belonged to Simon and Ruby.

Of course, Simon arrived early and had an eager look on his face. They enjoyed dinner and once again had great conversation.

"That was the best meal I have had in a long time," Simon said.

"I just put something together," Ruby said.

"Well, you put something good together," Simon said.

"What are we going to do," Simon asked.

"What do you mean," Ruby asked.

"I want to be with you, but I feel like you have reservations," Simon said.

"You are younger than I am, and you seem to be having money problems. I am not ready to go into something like that right now," Ruby said.

"The age doesn't have anything to do with it, and I will be okay with money," Simon said.

"I know I like you and I need you," Simon said. He didn't give Ruby a chance to say anything because he stood up and was standing in front of her gazing at her as if she was the most beautiful woman in the world. Ruby couldn't deny that it was something about him that immediately turned her on. He held out his hand and whispered to her, "let me take care of you."

Simon began to kiss her passionately and the way he looked at her, she couldn't explain how it made her feel. He kissed her neck and rubbed his hand over her throat and down to her breast. His big hands felt good over her body. She was so lost in his touch that she couldn't speak. He took her by the hand and led her upstairs. When they got to her bedroom, Simon whispered, "I want to take care of you." Simon gently unbuttoned her dress. Ruby was ready for this because she was completely naked.

Ruby began to take Simon's shirt off and started kissing his muscular chest. Simon was fine. He was really a dark beauty. He had a six-pack and he had a couple of tattoos. Tattoos turned Ruby on. She was so wet right now and she wanted him inside her. She unzipped his pants and she saw the biggest penis she had ever seen. Although they had made love in the hot tub, she really didn't get to see his body, but she did feel it. She just had no idea that his penis was this big. He was ready for her.

Ruby began kissing him from his chest to his penis. When she got there, she was in awe, but she put it in her mouth. It was huge, but she wet it and put it in her mouth and gave Simon probably the best blow job he ever had. He was feeling so good that he just kept saying, "Ruby, please don't stop." Ruby didn't stop and Simon returned the favor by lying Ruby's sexy body on the bed and giving her the best oral sex ever.

Simon finished his job as Ruby screamed for him to please make love to her. Simon turned her body over and entered her from behind. His thrust was so hard that it hurt, but felt good too. He was good and Ruby was having the time of her life. He turned her over, and he made love to Ruby and she forgot all her lost pain as this sexy man gave her the night of her life.

"You feel so good," Simon said as he was pounding harder and harder into Ruby.

"Oh, please, Oh, please," Simon said.

"I want you so bad," Ruby said.

"Please take this, please," Ruby said.

Simon was making love to Ruby and Ruby was feeling all of him inside of her. He had the biggest penis she had ever had in her life. It wasn't just big, it was good. Ruby was so Horney that Simon could feel the heat on his penis.

Simon could not believe this woman was so hot.

"Damn, baby this pussy good," he screamed over and over again.

Simon and Ruby made love for the rest of the night over and over again until their bodies were exhausted. They fell asleep in each other's arms. "Damn" was all the Ruby could say. She knew this wouldn't work, but the sex was good, so she just planned to play it out and let it do what it do.

CHAPTER 16

ॐ

THE next morning, Ruby got up before Simon and fixed breakfast. She was in another world for real. Thirty minutes earlier, Simon woke up and put his penis in her mouth and he gave her oral sex. Ruby could not remember the last time she did "69", but it was so good as they both climaxed together. He then turned her over and entered her from behind. At first, Ruby was scared because he had a big penis and she knew that it would not be pleasurable. Ruby was surprised because it fit right in and he felt so good.

"Oh, baby, this pussy is good," Simon said. Since they had gotten in the bedroom, those were the only words Simon had muttered.

It felt so good that Ruby couldn't say anything. She just gave it back to him as he gave it to her. She was making omelets and smiling the whole time. She was too old for this kind of sex, but damn it was good. She was in another zone when Simon sneaked in behind her. He was butt naked.

"Good morning, baby," Simon said.

"Hey, I was going to bring you breakfast in bed," Ruby said.

"Well, I will go back upstairs," Simon said. Simon turned Ruby around who was wearing a silk robe and one breast had found its way out. Simon began kissing Ruby gently and Ruby forgot all about the omelet. She just gave in as Simon liked her nipples as if they were his breakfast. She was turned on and she wanted more of that penis.

"Baby, this pussy good," Simon said as he slipped the robe off her naked, pretty body. Ruby turned around and cut the stove off and then jumped on the island. Simon proceeded down her body until he got to her wet, dripping pussy. It was wet like a sea of water. Simon opened her legs and went inside with his tongue. He was happy to be down there. He licked from one corner to another corner and Ruby was about to climax just from the licking, but she was trying to hold on.

"Simon, please eat my pussy," Ruby screamed. Simon obliged and gave Ruby the time of her life right there in her kitchen. He then asked her if he could have his way with her. She was not afraid because she wanted Simon to get all she had to offer. Simon and Ruby switched places and what happened next, Ruby had never experienced before in her life.

"Get on this dick," Simon said. Ruby jumped on him like an eager pupil. Simon told her to stand up on his penis. Ruby took her body and squatted on his penis and rode it like she was going crazy. This island was truly getting a work out. Simon and Ruby were throwing it back to each other until they both couldn't take it. They both exploded right there in the kitchen on the island. When it was over, Simon picked Ruby up and took her up the stairs. Ruby was in a state of shock and couldn't speak. She just rested her head on Simon. He took her to the bed and they lay there for the rest of the day. What happened to breakfast in bed? Hmmm.

CHAPTER 17

ᑫᖇ

Ruby and Simon stayed at the house all day. They ordered pizza and just chilled out. Ruby was trying not to like this man, but the penis had gotten her once again. Damon had Ashley. Ruby was stepping out the shower when the phone rang. It was Nathan.

"Hey sweet cakes," he said.

"I see your house is for sale, where are you," Nathan said.

"I moved away," Ruby said.

"Why, baby. As long as you know what the deal is," Nathan said.

"What do you want," Ruby said hastily.

"I want to see my favorite girl," Nathan said.

"Do you really think that I will ever see you again," Ruby said.

"Yes, baby. You know how we do it," Nathan said.

"I should have you and your partner in crime arrested," Ruby said as she was drying her wet body off.

"Look, you wouldn't want to do that because you wouldn't want anything to happen to Ashley," Nathan said.

Ruby didn't want to come off her high, so she just hung up the phone. Simon came from downstairs. Ruby couldn't even remember what he went downstairs for, but she knew her whole body shifted and she ran and jumped on him. She began passionately kissing him and he was thrown off guard, but he obliged. She forced Simon to the door and they went at it again. She was riding him as he was about to rub the paint off the wall. This was definitely the best sex Ruby had ever had.

"I have to go to work tomorrow," Ruby said as she fell back on the bed.

"I have to go to school tomorrow," Simon said.

"What are we suppose to do," Ruby asked.

"We have to act as if nothing is going on here," she said.

"I don't see what the big deal is when I am not your student," Simon said.

"The key point is that you are my student and we can't be seen like this because I need my job to pay for all this," Ruby said.

"I feel you," Simon said. They both were tired, but reality was a few hours around the corner. Ruby knew this could not be anything but sex and for the first time in her life, she was cool with that. She didn't want or need anybody as a full-time mate. She just hoped that Simon understood that.

Simon and Ruby slept and fucked the night away. The strangest thing is that they didn't seem to get tired of each other. However, whenever it's new or you're stealing it, it is always good.

The next morning Ruby got up early. She was ready to see her baby and she had a refreshing feeling.

"Good morning baby, "Simon said.

"Good morning. I am going to try to fix some breakfast," Ruby said.

"I guess I will let you finish this time," Simon said.

"Ok," Ruby said. Ruby was on cloud nine. She had forgotten all about the crazy stuff with Nathan and Camille and just focused on the good night she had with Simon. She tried to fix some omelets again. Maybe this time she wouldn't get distracted. Ruby had a smile on her face that she couldn't wipe off. Simon came down the stairs behind her and she could feel his hard-on.

"I am going to work today, so down boy," Ruby said. They ate and talked over breakfast. Simon left first. Ruby went over to her son's house to check on Ashley.

So, mom what was going on with you," Damon asked.

"Nothing, I just had some work I needed to catch up on," Ruby said.

"Oh, you just look like you gloating," Damon said.

"Well, maybe I am happy to see my favorite son," Ruby said.

"Yeah, right," Damon said. He told her that Ashley was still sleep and that his wife was off today too, so she could watch her until she came home this afternoon. Ruby agreed and went in to kiss her baby good-bye.

Ruby had bought a new convertible Mercedes and she had never driven it. She drove it today because she felt like letting the top down. She had a great night last night, but she didn't want to get involved with this man. For one, she was 50 years old and he was 26. Her son was 26. But it was something about Simon and he had gotten to Ruby.

CHAPTER 18

ᘓ

For the next two months, Ruby began spend a lot of time with Simon, but they were not dating. Simon was finishing his degree at the college, but he was not working. Ruby was enjoying Simon, but she was tired of him asking her for money. She was paying his rent and car payment as a loan. In Ruby's mind, a person can't get a loan without a job. Ruby felt it was time to have a conversation. Simon was upstairs sleeping and Ruby was ready to talk.

"So, what are we," Ruby asked as she was waking Simon up.

"What are you talking about," Simon said grudgingly.

"I want to know where we are in our relationship or is this a relationship," Ruby asked.

"I like you a lot, but I have some stuff I need to clear up," Simon said.

"Well, I feel like a girlfriend," Ruby said.

"What do you mean," Simon asked while he was trying to kiss Ruby on her neck.

"Look, I have been helping you out financially and if you have some loose ends , they should be helping you as well," Ruby said.

"I didn't know you felt that way," Simon said.

"Do you understand what I am saying," Ruby asked.

"Yeah, you think I am trying to use you, but I just need your help and those other women don't mean anything to me," Simon said.

"I don't want to argue about this, but I want to know where we are going," Ruby said.

"I want to be with you and I care a lot about you," Simon said.

Ruby had to think seriously about what he was saying because she wasn't sure what she wanted and he wasn't where he needed to be. What was she going to do? She didn't know, but right now she was about to make love to this man. She turned over to face Simon and she was immediately turned on. They began to passionately kiss and Ruby was ready for him to come inside of her. He slid her pants down and realized she was not wearing panties. He was getting super excited, and Ruby was in heat like crazy. Ruby climbed on top of Simon and it was on from there. Ruby got on top and rode Simon like she was crazy and for the next couple of minutes, she forgot about the bills and the money.

After Ruby and Simon had talked about the situation, Simon started staying away a little more. Ruby was busy at work because the college had lost an English faculty member and she had to teach more. She saw Simon a few times on campus and he had text that he needed to talk, but Ruby assumed his "loose ends" had him tied up.

By the end of the week, Simon called and said he wanted to take Ruby to dinner. Ruby called her son, so he could get Ashley for her and she was anxious to see what Simon had to say. He had made reservations at a nice restaurant downtown. Ruby had to admit when she walked in that Simon looked good. He had on a nice gray suit and his chocolate skin looked good next to the suit. Simon immediately stood up and pulled out a chair for Ruby.

"I really want to be your man," Simon said.

"I haven't seen you in awhile," Ruby said.

"I have had a lot of problems." Simon said.

"So you couldn't call, Ruby asked.

"I wanted to call, but I want to be the man that you need me to be," Simon said.

"I want to be with you, but I don't need drama or lies," Ruby said.

"I just need to get myself together," Simon said.

Ruby listened to Simon as he explained that he felt second-class because he wasn't up to par as she was. Ruby assured him that was the last thing that he needed to worry about because she liked him and she would help him all that she could.

Simon still hadn't found a job, so although he invited Ruby to dinner, Ruby ended with the bill. She was ok because she was set on a mission to help Simon be where he needed to be.

CHAPTER 19

ℭℛ

ABOUT three months had passed and Ruby was beginning to think that she was looking for jobs more than Simon was. He had several job interviews, but nothing came through. Ruby found out later that Simon had turned down a couple of jobs because according to him they were not right for him. Ruby didn't understand how a person could turn down a job and he didn't have one. Ruby continued to be patient, but her patience was running thin with Simon not having a job. He was enrolled at an online school, but Ruby was doing all the work, and he never asked about the progress of his classes. He just assumed that Ruby was taking care of everything.

With all the frustration and craziness, Ruby didn't even enjoy the sex, but Simon didn't even realize what was going on. Ruby was spending a lot of time with her son and her baby girl, but Simon never wanted to do family things with her. It was Fourth of July and Simon was at the house.

"We are having a cook out at my son's house and I would like for you to go," Ruby said.

"Baby, I really don't feel like being around anyone right now," Simon said.

"I would really like it if you would spend time with my family," Ruby said.

"I will, baby, but today I just want to chill," Simon said. Ruby didn't feel like fussing, so she just left with Ashley to go to the cook out .

Ruby went to the cook out and was miserable the whole time because everyone there seemed to be with their man, but her. Ruby knew it was a petty thing, but she wanted Simon to share family time with her. What really made Ruby mad was that when she got home, Simon was gone. He hadn't call or left a note, so she called his cell phone. When Ruby called the cell phone, it went straight to voice mail. Ruby couldn't do this---she was too old. Ruby took her shower and went to bed.

The next morning was Saturday and Ashley was up early. Ruby was up fixing breakfast when Simon was knocking on the door.

"What do you want," Ruby asked.

"I can explain. I fell asleep at a friend's house," Simon said.

"Why would you be at a friend's house when you didn't feel like going anywhere," Ruby asked.

"Look, I don't feel like this now, so can I just come in," Simon asked.

"I don't either, so go back wherever you were ," Ruby said as she slammed the door in his face.

"I am too old for this, Ruby screamed.

Ruby went about her day as she hit ignore on her phone several times from where Simon was calling ad texting. Ruby didn't care and she was not in the mood for the games. Ruby and Ashley went shopping and Ruby just tried to forget what happened with Simon. Ruby stayed in the mall for over two hours and as she was walking out Simon was standing by her car.

"What are you doing here," Ruby asked.

"I need you, and I am sorry," Simon said.

"I don't need someone who wants to play games and I feel like you are trying to play games," Ruby said.

"I have been right here for you, and you go and lie to me and get an attitude. I don't need you, and I will not be disrespected," Ruby said.

"Baby, I need you and I love you. I just need you to give me another chance," Simon said.

"I am so sorry for telling you a lie or not spending time with you and your family," Simon continued.

"I want you and I need you," Simon said. Ruby wondered if he needed her for her or all the things she had done for him.

"Let's go home, and let me show you," Simon said.

"I can't go through this with you. Either you want to be with me or you don't , but I can't go through all these changes," Ruby said.

"Just give me another chance," Simon said.

Ruby agreed and told him that she needed to get Ashley home. Simon followed her to the house and helped her get Ashley up to her bed. Ruby was tired and wanted a glass of wine. She headed downstairs to the kitchen and Simon was right behind her.

When they walked into the kitchen, Simon came up behind her and pushed her towards the island in the kitchen. Ruby had a on a halter top sundress and she was looking good, but Simon wasn't interested in the dress, he was interested in what was in the dress. He ripped the dress off her body and he was already hard. Her naked body had a glow from the window in the kitchen and it made Simon even more aroused. He entered her from behind and he could feel her juices flowing onto his penis and it made him want her even more. He was pounding inside of Ruby so hard that she thought she could feel his penis in her neck. He was giving it to her and she was giving it to him. It was so quick, yet so satisfying as they both climaxed right there in the kitchen. Ruby knew Simon wasn't good for her, but the sex was good. He knew he had her.

CHAPTER 20

ॐ

A YEAR had passed. Ashley was Ruby tried to do what she could to help Simon, but she was growing tired of him. He had found a job working as a supervisor in a local plant. He worked the night shift and slept most of the day. He was staying with Ruby because while he was out of work he lost his apartment. He was only supposed to be there a couple of months but it had been a year and he was still there.

Ruby was still doing Simon's online work, and he was still not participating. Demi was in Atlanta and was about to get married in three months, so Ruby was planning on going down and help with the planning. She had taken a couple of months off because she had been working so hard that she needed a break. Simon did not want her to go.

"Why do you have to go," Simon said.

"I have to help my daughter," Ruby said.

"You have plenty of time to work on the wedding," Simon said.

"Look, we are not discussing this because I am leaving tomorrow and I was just telling you," Ruby said.

"Well, I don't want you to go," Simon said.

"Simon, I will be back in two weeks. Is it that you want to go," Ruby asked.

"I can't go because I have to work," Simon said.

"Well, there is nothing that I can do about it, and I don't feel like talking about it again," Ruby said.

Simon didn't like Ruby's response and decided to stay with his mom while she was away. Ruby didn't care. Simon's mother was a superintendent of schools in the Los Angeles area. She was firm, but not very polite. Ruby had only met her twice since she had been dating Simon. She didn't seem to like Ruby and Ruby didn't care.

Ruby and Ashley flew to Atlanta the next day and Ruby didn't even tell Simon bye. She was tired of him, and when she got back, it was going to be some changes. For now, Ruby just wanted to enjoy Atlanta and Demi.

Ruby and Ashley arrived in Atlanta and it was something about Georgia. It was the fall of the year and the weather was perfect. Demi was glad to see her mom and her sister. Demi followed in her mom's footsteps and she was a college professor but she taught chemistry and she was about to marry her college sweetheart, Chris. He was from New Mexico and they had met when Demi was a freshman. He was an engineer. He was a nice guy and Ruby really liked him.

Demi and Ruby did a lot of shopping over the next couple of days while Ashley tagged along. Demi didn't know that Ruby was dating a younger man, so she was inquiring about her mom's love life. After walking around in three malls, it was time to eat. They decided to go to Ted Turner's restaurant downtown. The food was good, and they even saw Ted Turner. Ashley had fallen asleep, so Demi and Ruby played catch up.

"So, mom how's your love life," Demi asked.

"You mean your brother hasn't told you anything," Ruby said.

"I know a couple of times I called him, Ashley was there," Demi said.

"Yes, he helps me out sometimes when I have things to do," Ruby said.

"So, is there someone in your life," Demi asked.

"I have a friend, but it's not serious," Ruby said.

"Why, you need to be with someone," Demi said.

"Well, I am really ok. I have my job, my friends, and my money," Ruby said.

Demi and Ruby both just started laughing while they finished their lunch. As Demi and Ruby were leaving the restaurant, Ruby noticed that Simon had called seven times and had left some crazy text messages. She wasn't in the mood, so she just cut her phone off.

CHAPTER 21

ᏣᎡ

Ruby stayed in Atlanta for the next couple of days. She had bought Demi a big house, so there was plenty of room for Ashley and her to stay. While Demi was at work, Ashley and Ruby would shop for the wedding and themselves. Ruby was really enjoying Atlanta and she was regretting going back to California and facing Simon. Ruby had agreed to meet with some old friends at college. One of her friends, Christie was an attorney and her other friend, Jake, was one of Ruby's old flames. Jake was also an English professor at Spellman. Ruby knew Jake was probably loving the women there and having him some fun on the side too.

They met at a nice restaurant and had a couple of drinks as they reminisced about the old days. Jake had been married twice. He was recently divorced. Ruby remembered they had some good times in college and he still looked good. He had three children, but they were grown. Christie had just gotten married for the first time at 50 a year ago. She was enjoying life. She had married another attorney.

Jake kept looking at Ruby, but Ruby was on cloud nine. She had three drinks and two drinks were her limit. Jake wanted Ruby and she could see it in his eyes.

"So, where are you staying," Jake asked.

"I am staying with my daughter," Ruby said.

"When is the wedding," Christie asked.

"It will be in December, Christmas Eve," Ruby said.

"That should be nice," Christie said.

"So, you will be back," Jake said.

"Several times," Ruby said.

"So, I thought you had a baby," Jake said.

"She is six and she is with my other daughter," Ruby said.

"Did you ever find out who killed your husband," Jake asked.

Ruby almost went in to shock and she couldn't speak.

"I am sorry, Ruby, I didn't mean to upset you," Jake said.

"It's just been a minute since I have talked about it, and no we never found out," Ruby said.

"Is that why you moved," Jake asked. Christie interrupted by saying that Jake was asking too many questions, but Ruby told it was okay.

"I couldn't really stay in the house knowing my husband was killed in my front yard. It was hard, but I had to do what I had to do and I love California. Christie had to leave, so Jake and Ruby stayed and chatted. Simon had called a couple of times, but Ruby hit ignore. Ruby needed to stay around the restaurant to sober up because she was feeling good.

"It's really good to see you," Jake said.

"It's good to see you too. I saw you on Face Book a couple of times, but we never chatted," Ruby said.

"I know. It's been really crazy with my last divorce," Jake said. I have just had a hard time with this last divorce, Jake said.

Ruby was checking Jake out. He was so fine. He was tall, dark and handsome just like Simon but Jake didn't have this extra baggage. He had the prettiest white teeth with a gold crown in the corner. As he was talking, all Ruby could do was look at his smile. Ruby didn't know what made her say this, but she said it.

"Can we go back to your place," Ruby asked."

Hell yes," Jake said. "Are you sure,", he asked.

"Please take me back to your place," Ruby said.

Ruby was in a rental car, so they left it at the restaurant and rode in Jake's convertible Mercedes. It was very nice. Ruby was feeling so good. They drove for about 15 minutes until they were in this subdivision in Lithonia. Ruby assumed he was staying in an apartment since he was recently divorced.

"So, you got the house," Ruby asked,"

"No, she got the one we bought together, but I already had this one," he said. It was a nice two-story house. Ruby got out after Jake and for the next couple of minutes or hours, she wanted to forget Simon and all the crazy things that had been going on.

When they got into the house, Jake was unsure how to proceed, so he tried to make small talk, but Ruby cut him short.

"Let's not pretend and just enjoy the moment," Ruby said.

Jake took her hand upstairs and led her to his bedroom. When they got to the bedroom, he began to kiss Ruby on her neck and he was whispering how he had thought of her often. Ruby didn't respond. It had been twenty years since she had been with Jake. But from what she remembered, if he still had it, it was good. He had great hands and he was running them all over her body. Ruby had been having sex with Simon, but it wasn't good anymore because of the stress behind it. Anyway, right now, she wanted Jake inside of her.

He turned Ruby around so that she was facing him and he gave her one of the most passionate kisses she had in a long time. Simon was not a good kisser, but she had to get him out of her mind because right now she was about to give all of herself to Jake.

Ruby was wearing a nice fitted top with some cute jeans. Jake gently took her top off while he was continued to kiss her as if he hadn't kissed a woman in a long time. She kissed him back as if she hadn't kissed a man in a long time. Everything was so passionate. He slid her jeans off and Ruby wasn't even wearing any underwear.

"Were you expecting me," Simon said.

"Maybe, so," Ruby said.

"Damn, your body is perfect," Simon said. Ruby helped Jake take off his clothes and he still had the six pact and he still looked good. Damn was the only thing she could think of. He looked so good…He continued kissing her and then he stopped and asked, "Can I do whatever I want?"

"Hell yes," Ruby screamed. She was so horny and ready for him to enter her. He went down on Ruby and no one had ever gone down on her like that before. He was giving her oral sex like this was really his lunch. Ruby had climaxed twice when he got up and she saw he still was hanging. He still had it going on.

He reached on the night stand to put on his condom and then he turned Ruby around and told her to get on her knees. She obeyed and he slid his big penis into her from behind and she literally screamed. He was stroking it nice and slow and Ruby was so hot that she was throwing it back and screaming out obscenities. She was on fire and he was putting it out. Ruby was begging him to stop because she was about to climax again, but he was just getting started. He turned her around and he entered her from the front and he really began to make love to Ruby. He was kissing and grinding and kissing and grinding. He was on it. He was talking back to Ruby and that was making Ruby hotter. They were so into it that that they were both hot and sticky and they were about to climax together. It was wonderful. Ruby was exhausted as Jake rolled off her. Neither could speak and they fell asleep butt naked until Ruby's phone rang. She rolled over to see who it was and it was Simon. She hit ignore and set him a text message. She rolled back over, and Jake hadn't move. He was sleep with a smile on his face.

Ruby called Demi and told her that she was still with friends and she would be out for awhile. Demi told her that she and Ashley had been out shopping for the wedding and that Ashley was knocked out. Ruby got up to take a shower because she needed one more round with Jake. He rose to get up too and told her that her parking bill was going to be hell, but Ruby said she didn't care.

She proceeded to the shower and so did Jake. He continued his pleasure in the shower and they made love over and over again until it was around midnight. Jake begged Ruby to stay, but she wanted to go home, so he drove her back to her car and they agreed to stay in touch.

Ruby wasn't sure if she would see Jake again or not. She knew for the moment that he had served his purpose and he had done well. Now, she had to deal with Simon. So after she took a shower, she called him. He answered.

"What the hell is going on," Simon said.

"I have been so busy and I told you that when I came here," Ruby said.

"So busy, you couldn't pick up your phone," Simon said.

"Well, don't you say that sometimes when you don't pick up," Ruby said.

"So, now you want to play games," Simon said.

"No, I am just keeping it real," Ruby said.

"Why are you calling so late," Simon said.

"I just got a chance," Ruby said.

"What is really going on? You have been gone for a couple of weeks and you haven't talked to me, just texting. And then, what about my work online," Ruby said.

"Oh, you are worried about the work online, I didn't think you cared," Ruby said.

"Look, I am tired and I don't want to argue, so when are you coming home," Simon said.

"I will be back this weekend, "Ruby said.

"And we need to talk," Ruby said.

"So, you will be back Friday or Saturday," Simon said.

"Probably Saturday," Ruby said.

"Well, I have been staying with Mom and I wanted to know if I could go to the house," Simon said.

"Yes, that is fine," Ruby said. She really didn't want him to, but she figured that he already had been there. There were going to be some changes soon....very soon.

"Ok, well I do love you," Simon said.

"Ok, I love you too," Ruby said. She thought she did at one time, but now things were different—very different.

CHAPTER 22

CR

O VER the next couple of days, Ruby and Demi finalized their last plans and Ruby agreed to come back in a month which would be October to do the final arrangements and planning. It was Friday and Ruby decided to go home early. She changed her flight and Demi took her to the airport. They had fun, but it was time to go. Ruby was homeschooling Ashley and they had been off track for a minute. So, Ruby and Ashley were headed back to California. Ruby forgot to call Simon to let him know she would be home early, but it was okay. She would talk to him when she got in.

Ruby and Ashley slept most of the way back and when they did wake up, they were in California. With the time difference, Ruby was a little exhausted. She had Damon pick her up at the airport and Ashley wanted to go with him, so Damon dropped Ruby off and she saw Simon was there. Damon offered to take her bags in, but Ruby said she was okay.

She got all her stuff in, and she didn't see Simon, so she went upstairs. She could hear water running, but when she got upstairs, she saw clothes on the floor-Simon's and a woman's. She heard giggles in the shower.

Ruby's heart was pounding faster. She knew that Simon did not have a woman in HER house. She opened the door and there was Simon giving it to some woman in HER shower. She quickly pulled the shower curtain back and grabbed at Simon. The woman was screaming and hollering and trying to run away. Ruby was choking Simon and trying to drown him in the shower, but this whore was not getting away. She ran behind her and through her down the stairs. Her naked body splashed on Ruby's hardwood floors. Blood was everywhere.

Simon came running down the stairs naked and dripping.

"What have you done," Simon screamed.

"How the hell could you have someone in my house fucking her in my bathroom," Ruby screamed. Ruby was grabbing at Simon, but he was trying to run away from her.

"Who the hell is this woman," Ruby said.

"Whoever she is, you just killed her," Simon screamed.

"Well, if she came to my house to fuck my man, she wanted to die," Ruby shouted.

"What are you going to do, this woman is dead," Simon screamed.

"Well, it should be you," Ruby said as she ran upstairs.

When Ruby came back downstairs, she had her gun and everybody was going to die. Simon was kneeling beside this dead woman trying to revive her.

"She is dead," Ruby said.

"Just like you should be," Ruby said.

"You are crazy. You can't kill a person, and act like you don't know what is going on," Simon said.

"This is what I know. You had a bitch in my house fucking her in my bathroom. You don't pay any bills here, you don't have any right bringing someone in my house. You are fucking crazy," Ruby said.

"You said you were coming back on Saturday," Simon said.

"You stupid son of a bitch," Ruby shouted. She couldn't take it anymore. She took out her gun as he was turned toward the door and shot him in the head. His lifeless body fell over the woman on the floor.

Ruby had to think quick and she couldn't stop crying. She didn't know what to do, but she had to get two bodies out her house. She couldn't breathe----she couldn't think. She ran to the kitchen and got a glass of wine. A thousand things were running through her head. She didn't know what to do or who to call.

Her first instinct was to put both bodies in the car and leave it somewhere. Ruby went to check on the bodies...they were still there... lifeless. Then, she went upstairs to take a shower, but she couldn't use the one in her room. She used the guest bathroom and then she changed into some jogging clothes. Ruby went back downstairs and put Simon's clothes on. He was so heavy, but Ruby had gained some immeasurable strength. She put his clothes on, and put his body in his car. He then dressed the woman and she realized she knew her. She had been a student in her class and she worked at the gym.

Something had gotten into Ruby because she wasn't even mad anymore. She was just ready to get them out her house. She immediately thought about Nathan and Camille. If they could get away with murder, she sure could. She wiped their bodies down, so her prints wouldn't be anywhere on them.

Ruby drove about an hour away to a park and hid the car in the back woods close to the park. It was dark, so she had to be careful. She put Simon's body in the front seat and she put the woman, whose name was Angela, in the passenger seat.

Ruby had to be careful, so she jogged all the way back home. It took her awhile, but she was physically fit. Ruby got back and put her plan in motion. Soon as she got home, she had to clean her foyer of the blood and make sure there was nothing left out of place. She had placed Simon's cell phone and Angela's purse in the car. She then called Simon's mother.

"Hey, I have been trying to call Simon and I haven't heard from him," Ruby said.

"He left this morning and said he had to drive over to San Francisco, but I haven't heard from him," Simon's mother said.

"Okay, well if you do hear from him, tell him to call me," Ruby said.

Perfect. No one knew that he was there. For the next couple of weeks, things were sort of crazy because Simon's mom reported him missing and the police was at the college and even at Ruby's house. The only person who saw Simon's car that day was Damon. He did ask his mom about it, but she told him that he left right after she got there.

Ruby went to the funeral and played the sad girlfriend. It did bother Ruby that this did not affect her. She didn't feel anything but anger. She cried at the funeral because she was angry at Simon for disrespecting her and her house. After the funeral, Simon's mom was clinging to Ruby for moral support. This was her only child. She was beyond hurt. She was just in turmoil. Ruby tried to console her, but she was just ready for this to be over.

Ruby carried her life for the next couple of months. She went back to Atlanta and helped Demi with her wedding. Of course, she met up with Jake and had great sex. He tried to have a relationship, but Ruby was done with that part of her life. She enjoyed life and felt no remorse. The police came up with a couple of theories, but nothing that related back to Ruby, so she just lived her life as she had done before.

CHAPTER 23

❦

FIVE years later, Ashley had turned ten years old. She was very active and kept Ruby busy. Demi was doing well in Atlanta and Damon and Ruby saw each other almost every day. They never solved Simon's case and that hurt his mom a lot. She stayed at the police station trying to make them do some work. Ruby figured the City of California had better things to do.

Ruby found out that she had cancer and realized it that her sickness may be her karma. However, she was at peace with what she had done. Ruby was dying and she told her children what was going on, so they could be prepared and Demi was pregnant, but told her mom she would take Ashley.

Ruby had heard that Camille was killed in a car wreck and her son was severely injured. Ruby also heard that Nathan's wife had caught him with her sister and killed them both. She got life in prison. Ruby thought how lucky or cursed she had been. She had gotten away with murder but to her it was for two people who deserved it.

Ruby died at the age of 65. Ashley found her one morning in her bed. She had an elaborate funeral. She had a pink casket topped with beautiful pink carnations. Flowers were sent from near and far. Demi, Damon, and Ashley had each other and they did the best they could do to hold up in a time like this. It was a sad occasion, but for Ruby she was ready. Ruby had done everything she wanted to do in life and she felt her children would be all right. She had loved and lost and lost and loved. Love or life didn't owe her anything. Rest in peace, Dr. Ruby.